"What Happened When I Died?"

She looked at him long and sadly. "You are a phantom out of my past. You are a walking dead man. You are an abomination—and yet, I hunger at the sight of your face."

"I still love you."

"Shut up!"

"I do."

Tears were flowing freely down her face, but she remained unchanged.

"Shashi, what did you come here for?"

"To ask you, in memory of the man who once wore that sweet body, in the name of the man you think yourself to be, to leave me and mine utterly alone. Never to seek me out. Never to contact my son. Not to haunt me like the ghost that you are."

"My God, Shashi. Do you know what you're asking? He's my son, too."

A FOND FAREWELL TO DYING

SYD LOGSDON

A TIMESCAPE BOOK

PUBLISHED BY POCKET BOOKS NEW YORK

A portion of this novel was previously published in a slightly different form in the June 1978 issue of *Galaxy Magazine* under the title "To Go Not Gently" copyright © 1978 by UPD Publishing Company.

Another *Original* publication of TIMESCAPE BOOKS

A Timescape Book published by
POCKET BOOKS, a Simon & Schuster division of
GULF & WESTERN CORPORATION
1230 Avenue of the Americas, New York, N.Y. 10020

ISBN: 0-671-41099-7

First Timescape Books printing March, 1981

10 9 8 7 6 5 4 3 2 1

TIMESCAPE and design are trademarks of Simon & Schuster.
POCKET and colophon are trademarks of Simon & Schuster.

Printed in the U.S.A.

Author's Note

The rescue techniques used in the opening of Chapter 31 are correctly portrayed. C.P.R. administered by laymen saves lives every day. You can learn it from your local chapter of the American Red Cross or the American Heart Association.

S. L.

Oh, threats of Hell and Hopes of Paradise!
One thing at least is certain—This Life flies;
  One thing is certain and the rest is Lies;
The Flower that once has bloomed forever dies.

—*Khayyám/FitzGerald*

1.

He will take up his pen to make notes. The experiment progressing well, he will write, in past tense, ". . . 3.762 liters of sterile H_2O were introduced into the solution . . .", though the events he describes are ongoing. Caught up in a labyrinth of language, he will be unable to comprehend non-linear time. This will be, will have been, and will become the driving force in his life.

2.

In the five million years of his groping, evolving existence, only once had man changed more than the superficial appearance of his world (for the transplantation, augmentation, and destruction of species is of no consequence in the life of continents). Even then he merely hurried by a few millennia a process already well under way.

When thirty-two thermonuclear devices struck the western coast of North America in the same millisecond of geological time, the delicate balance of faults was disturbed. In that same millisecond—or in the next two centuries, as man measures time—the subsidence was completed and the Pacific tectonic plate had moved fourteen kilometers to the northwest and a hundred meters closer to the core of the earth, opening the Gulf of California from end to end.

A minor change, to be sure, and brought about by only a fraction of the energy expended in the death throes of the circum-Atlantic nations. But sufficient. Deep oceanic currents changed; some species perished while others flourished and new ones were born of mutations. The ice caps diminished. The sea rose. Salt water covered the crater where the Vatican had stood.

Gone was the Central Valley of California and the Willamette Valley of Oregon; in the eastern United States, only the Applachians and the Ozarks remained exposed. The radioactive ruin of the industrial northeast was mercifully hidden from the eyes of man, as was most of Europe and the Amazonian basin.

India became an island as the mighty valleys of the Panch-ab and the Ganga were inundated. There would be no more border incidents with Pakistan; there was no more Pakistan, and her citizenry fled westward to the new pan-Islamic nation of Medina. China and Russia pounded one another into oblivion, Europe was utterly destroyed, and India stepped in to pick up the pieces.

No one bothered to conquer what was left of North America.

For two centuries, broken, bleeding, half-sterilized mankind had refrained from its ultimate weapon; now men were once again prepared to hurl nuclear death at their neighbors.

3.

IMAGES:

Nirghaz Husain looks out of his hotel window, up into the perfect blue sky, and curses. Steely arrows of death, planes of the Indian Air Force, lace the sky with their contrails; now dipping to deliver their bombs; now fleeing skyward pursued by Medinan missiles. Husain shakes his head in disbelief. How could he have ordered an airstrike now? How could he!

Then one deathdart (type XKX9, designation Yama) tears the air overhead and Husain's disbelief dissolves into pain.

IMAGES:

A Medinan agent deep in India grinds his teeth as he hears the news of Sri Karji's "preemptive airstrike". He turns momentarily from his fellow workers to master his expression, then returns to the construction of the speaker's podium where Kantikar is scheduled to speak some weeks hence.

IMAGES:

Two scientists at the Institute of Advanced Biological Research in Poona attend the birth of a unique bottle-nosed dolphin and transfer him immediately to a sensory deprivation tank. Intent on their work, they miss the news broadcast, but the newstats will be full of it later. Then Ram David Singh will sit with the stat forgotten in his lap, thinking back to his boyhood in Ozarka and to the questions of life and death that had seemed so certain then, but which had haunted him from that day to this.

IMAGES:

A Medinan general sits before a viewscreen, waiting, wondering; an Indian general paces behind a battery of technicians, waiting, wondering; and the nuclear missiles each general controls lie quiescent, waiting, not wondering, but sure.

IMAGES:

Jogendranath Kantikar, premier of all India, Sri Karji to the followers who revere him, sits in a dimly lighted office bearing on his thin shoulders all the despair, the agony, and the guilt of a world leader who has erred grievously. And of a parent who has destroyed the life of his child.

PART I

India—2202 A.D.

Chapter 1

RAM DAVID SINGH, BORN DAVID SINGER in the island state of Ozarka, in NorAm, shifted his position and apologized to the man he had jostled. He was rewarded for that small courtesy by a flashing smile and a deprecating comment in Bengali. Dave had some trouble assimilating the reply, though his command of NaiHind should theoretically have allowed him to converse at least haltingly in any one of twelve languages including Bengali and Sanskrit. The Bengali had said, "It was nothing"; and it had been nothing by Indian standards, but Dave had never accustomed himself to crowding. Physical and emotional distance were both a part of NorAm culture, and he had never become more Indian than politeness dictated.

To gain this vantage point on the hill overlooking the podium, Dave had come twenty-four hours early and had camped with sandwiches and a sleeping bag. Now he wondered if that had been wise, for as the morning advanced the crowd redoubled and his discomfort grew. He began to understand how India must have been in the late twentieth century before radiation-induced barrenness had halved the birth rate.

Beyond the podium the dyke arrowed away toward the northeast, gray-brown and unimpressive save for its incongruity. It was the mightiest engineering feat in the history of mankind, yet that which could be seen was only a hundred-meter-wide strip of smooth magma-stone stretching from the shore out to sea, where it was lost in the curvature of the earth. One could look at it and be unimpressed, but only if one were ignorant that that line of magmastone ran unbreached for more than eight hundred kilometers.

Soon the pumps would start their work and the seawater which covered the fertile valley of the Ganges would begin to be expelled. It would take a decade, even with two dozen fusion-powered pumping stations. The central pumping station would continue for as long as mankind inhabited the valley, taking the waters of the mighty Mother Ganga where they reached the seawall and redirecting them to irrigate vast stretches of the Deccan.

The crowd drawn up on the beach was dazzling to the eye. Kantikar gripped the edge of the podium as he looked out at them, exhilarated. They spread away like an endless sea—his people. Once his country had been filled up with teeming millions. Now there were but few remaining, and to see so many gathered together was worth a lifetime of effort.

Sterility had spread across the earth with the clouds of fallout following the Cataclysm. It had claimed Europe entirely, and much of northern Asia. India had escaped the worst of the plague, shielded by the bulwark of the Himalayas. Still, each year saw fewer births than deaths. At first it had been a blessing, but that time was far past.

Kantikar moved on across the platform, making way for the attendants carrying his grandson's wheelchair.

Nirghaz Husain had been an athlete before he lost his legs in the bombing of Mahmet. It hurt Kantikar to see him crippled, but the ingrown bitterness in Husain's face hurt him even more.

Sri Karji was loved and hated with equal fervor. Jogendranath Kantikar; Sri Jogendranath Kantikarji when the honorifics were added—out of affection and practicality his followers had shortened it to Sri Karji. He was a descendant of Gopal Kantikar, the man who had led India during the turbulent years after the Cataclysm when she had emerged as *the* world power. Sri Karji's party had remained in power for the last two decades by maintaining a moderate policy toward Medina, even while his detractors called for immediate war over the Panch-ab dispute.

Someone in a dark suit came up and spoke quickly, *"Eek, doo, teen, char!"* testing the sound equipment. Husain settled himself in to watch while Kantikar argued briefly with his aides. Visibly reluctant, they lowered the armored glass so that he could face the crowd unprotected. A ripple of approval spread through the throng.

Sri Karji placed his hands together and bowed slightly; his, "Namaste," was drowned by wild shouting that went on for ten minutes. Finally, the crowd settled down enough that his amplified voice could be heard.

"Friends, we have come together to celebrate the completion of a great labor. Our people have worked together to clear away the sea that covers the Ganges, the great Mother Ganga, but in our moment of celebration we must not forget what has happened in the Panch-ab."

Since the perfection of magmastone as a dam-building material, India had reclaimed the valleys of the Narmada, the Tapti, the Godavri, the Mahanadi, and the Krishna. Then, a decade earlier, Kantikar had presided at a similar celebration at the completion of the massive dam between Udaipur and NaiHyderabad, six hundred kilometers of magmastone and a dozen pumping stations. Only the Ganga project was larger. In the succeeding decade the Panch-ab project had begun to drain the valley of the five rivers of western India.

India had gained new lands, but the Muslim nation of Medina had also begun to move in where the waters receded from their territory, claiming what had been Pakistan. India and Medina had never viewed one another with favor; in fact, the dispute had really begun with the first Muslim invasion of the Indian subcontinent 1,200 years earlier, and seemed unlikely ever to die down.

Kantikar spoke with fervor against the Medinans, castigating them for taking lands freed by the Panch-ab project. The crowd went wild with each new proclamation. Kantikar had chosen an auspicious moment to initiate his toughened policy toward Medina. These were the same people who had reacted so favorably to Kantikar's preemptive airstrike against the Medinan city of Mahmet, built on the ruins of old Lahore after they were exposed by the Panch-ab project.

There was a shot—a high, brittle bark. Kantikar fell back among his aides, struck down by the impact, and further bullets ripped the bulwark surrounding the podium.

The guards returned fire at the rifleman, regardless of the crowd around him. Those innocents surrounding the assassin scattered, crushing into the arms of their fellows, and a wave of motion swept through the crowd like liquid.

Then Kantikar staggered to his feet, holding his bleeding shoulder with his opposite hand. He turned to the microphone and shouted to the crowd to be calm. One of the guards tried to pull him down, but Kantikar shrugged him off; a spectator emerged from the crowd shouting that he was a doctor and the guards restrained him, not knowing for certain that he was what he claimed. An official doctor came running. Husain strained helplessly in his wheelchair while Kantikar spoke angrily with the knot of security personnel surrounding him, then turned back to the microphone.

"Friends!" At his preliminary expression the crowd fell silent, save for the guards who were carrying away the assassin and the bodies of those unfortunates who had been standing near him. "Bear with me, for the pain is considerable.

"I came here to speak on the problems our nation faces today. I feel sure that this assassination attempt was but another attempt by our enemies in Medina to destroy our nation. Their inheritance of perfidy stretches back for more than a millennium, and there is no reason to think that they will change their ways in the foreseeable future.

"Ten years ago we began draining the Panch-ab to regain land for ourselves and our children. No sooner had the sea begun to recede than Medinan squatters began to settle on the new land—Indian land. For a decade we negotiated, protested, and even fought occasional skirmishes. Only the fear of loosing another cataclysm has held us back from administering justice to the thieves from Medina.

"For ten years we forbore, and what did they do? They built their farms and cities on our land!

"As you know, three months ago I ordered airstrikes against the city of Mahmet. The Medinans accused us of committing an act of war, but it was not such, for Mahmet lies on Indian soil.

"Claiming false righteousness, the Medinans have spread lies to the world at large that we are warmongers. Today their true nature stands revealed."

He paused, hanging his head. The blood was bright against his white tunic. When he continued, his voice was weaker. "Today I came to tell you that our patience is growing thin, and we are not prepared to relinquish *one square meter* of Indian soil to any invader. And that we will take whatever measures are necessary to prevent such thievery!"

As he turned away from the microphone, the crowd

went wild with applause and cheering. It seemed to go on forever, dying slightly, then redoubling as the ambulance roared away with the wounded premier inside.

Another figure mounted the podium; it was the administrator of the Ganga project, though few of those in the crowd recognized him. The cheering went on, shifting subtly, then suddenly to cries of, *"Jai Hind! Jai Hind! Jai Hind!"* The chant rolled echoes against the hillside and the crowd surged in waves and undulations. The administrator finally gave up making himself heard and motioned to the staff behind him. Somehow the signal was passed to the technicians in their bunkers and, a kilometer out at sea, the first pumping station broke into action; simultaneously, all the other pumping stations began, but they were lost around the curvature of the earth.

From its exit broke a stream of water, fifty meters through and arrowing slantwise skyward for two hundred meters before breaking up and falling back to the sea with the sound of a waterfall and the pyrotechnic brilliance of a captive rainbow.

The sound of the crowd grew even louder, and the same cry that had accompanied mobs in Calcutta in the 1940s as they demanded independence from Britain echoed and re-echoed from the hillsides, an audible challenge to the eternal enemy, Medina.

"Jai Hind!"

Chapter 2

IT SEEMED TO DAVE THAT EVERYONE IN India had come to watch the opening of the flow, and the airport at Ranchi was choked. Air India had scheduled extra flights, and it was one of these that he boarded at three A.M. after a ten-hour wait in the terminal.

It deposited him in Bombay as the sun was rising. Bombay had not been lost to either fire or flood, but had gradually grown up the mountainside as the sea level rose. The ocean had inundated old Bombay first, then the earliest of the post-Cataclysm buildings. What remained was a somewhat chaotic, but utterly new, city which still maintained some continuity with what it had been.

Dave settled down on a bench in the sun outside the station, waiting for the monorail to Poona and enjoying the panorama of Indian life. It was a colorful, sensual crowd. He watched the mothers with babies on their hips, their full breasts straining their *choties*. Since the

Cataclysm, barrenness had become the norm, and women who were able to bear children had become a rare and treasured commodity, with a resultant shift in values of beauty.

Aboard the train, Dave settled back and looked out across the dry countryside at the peasant farmers working their poor fields. The sterility that had reversed mankind's growth rate had also affected his crops, so that the same old precarious balance between food and births still existed.

Dave had grown up on such a farm, in NorAm, and had only left when his father died. Two days later he was heading out as a deckhand on a costal schooner.

All of the major ships were driven by fusion piles. Natural hydrocarbons were long since used up and synthetic replacements were prohibitively expensive. The minor trade that was beneath the notice of the big shipping companies was carried on by small sailing craft, mostly ferroconcrete with sails of various glass fiber synthetics. Sea travel was more important than ever now that large portions of the monolithic continents were inundated.

Dave had stayed in the costal trade for two years, advancing to mate on a medium-sized yawl, but the education he had only halfheartedly followed rose up to haunt him. He left his ship in Roanoke on the coast of Appalachia. Outside of Calgary, Roanoke boasted the finest college in NorAm. There he worked as a stevedore, and, later, harbor pilot, as he studied biology.

For two years after he got his degree, he studied the northward extension of mule deer populations into the now temperate barrens, but he was not satisfied. The NorAm universities were strictly third rate, and it soon became apparent to Dave that he did not have the training to do the job he had set out to do.

Much of the world was in turmoil. Africa was seething, with the black nations of the center pitted against the white nations of the south and the white refugee nations of the Saharan plains. Europe was a broken cinder. Asia, north of the Himalayas, was in the midst of a new dark age, made worse by the circumpolar band of mutations. What remained of South America was under the sure and heavy hand of the New Vatican, locked into the mold of a neo-Catholic, neo-Incan culture. NorAm was fighting its unsteady way back from barbarism. Only one nation retained both personal freedom and a technological culture— India—and it was to India that Dave chose to go.

He could not afford public transportation, nor could he find work on one of the gigantic nuclear cargo ships; they would have no place for either a second-rate biologist or a deckhand knowing only sailing ships. So Dave bought a small crabbing boat, re-rigged it for a long passage, and left Juneau sailing south and west. Seven months later he sold the now decrepit craft for salvage in Bombay and hiked to Poona, where he took a job as a lab assistant at Deccan University and began to study NaiHind in earnest. Six months later he enrolled in classes.

Six years later, India was his home and he was Professor Ram David Singh of the Institute of Advanced Biological Research, Deccan University, Poona, of the last civilized nation on earth.

Tasmeen interrupted Dave in mid-morning. He was in his favorite position—lounging in a decrepit armchair in the corner of his lab, reading a journal with his bare feet on the windowsill intercepting the morning breeze.

"Someone to see you in your office, Professor."

"Send him in here."

"I think you had better go to him," she replied, eyeing the rubble about her with mock distaste. Dave shrugged, slipped into sandals, and followed.

The reason for Tasmeen's unusual solicitude was

soon apparent. Dave's visitor was in a wheelchair. He was small featured and handsome, with a sober air, and the lap robe did nothing to disguise his leglessness.

"Professor Singh, this is Sri Nirghaz Husain. Sri Husain, Professor Ram David Singh."

Dave did *namaste,* touching his hands together before his chest and bobbing his head in a greeting which Husain returned. "What can I do for you, Sri Husain?"

Husain looked faintly embarrassed. "I was told that you are the director of the Institute?"

Dave nodded. "Yes, although that may not entail what you think." He pulled up a chair and sat opposite Husain. Tasmeen returned with tea.

"Now, Sri Husain, you have to understand what it is to be the director of this Institute. We are all researchers here, and need no one to tell us what to do; the director simply shuffles paperwork and sees to it that the rest of us have money to work with. That's all. Each one of us takes his turn as director on a bi-yearly rotation, and my term of servitude is up in a few days. Then Professor Mukerjee will be director, poor man."

Husain smiled despite himself. "You are not an Indian?"

"NorAm by extraction; Indian by citizenship and inclination."

"But still NorAm in your informality."

Dave smiled. "Perhaps. What can the Institute do for you, Sri Husain?"

Husain's brows came together and he hesitated. "I understand that you are on the forefront of regeneration research?"

Suddenly Dave understood his reticence. "Your legs?"

"Yes."

"I'm sorry, Sri Husain, but I doubt that there is anything we can do for you. If we were able to regenerate human parts, you can be sure that it would be on all the news channels. We are working toward that end, and one of our members feels that she may be fairly close, but the techniques have not been proved."

"I am willing to take a chance, Dr. Singh, if the odds are at all favorable. To be so confined is intolerable."

Dave leaned back, drumming his fingers, then called out to Tasmeen. She stuck her head in and he said, "Ask Dr. Mathur to step in if she can break away." When she had gone he turned back to Husain. "As I said, my role as director is a small one. Dr. Mathur is the expert on regeneration. You must understand, however, that our purpose here is to find techniques to overcome sterility. Regeneration research is directed primarily toward that end."

Shashi Mathur stepped in moments later with a smile for Dave which she quickly hid. *Proper British formality lives on in India long after Britain is but a memory.* Dave introduced them and she said, "Sri Husain? Sri Nirghaz Husain?"

He nodded and Dave looked blank. "Sri Husain is a famous polo player," Shashi prompted. Dave caught her momentary hesitation over tense. "He is also the grandson of Sri Karji."

Suddenly, a light dawned. The Premier, Jogendranath Kantikar; Sri Karji. His grandson, Nirghaz Husain, had been the chief negotiator for India in its disputes with Medina over the land recovered by the Panch-ab project.

Dave's embarrassment was written across his face and Husain chuckled. "I thought that sequestered men of science were purely fictional."

"No, I'm afraid that we are very real," Dave admitted. He studiously avoided newscasts, but the more spectacular stories always managed to trickle through his defenses. Nirghaz Husain was the son of Sri Karji's youngest daughter and a Muslim father. She had left home at an early age, creating a scandal that Sri Karji's parliamentary opponents would not let die, but had returned to India with her son after the Medinan Muslims had made life intolerable for her.

Her son by Parivar Husain had gone back to Medina upon his father's death to inherit his fortune and act as an unofficial emissary between Sri Karji and the Muslims. He had been there when the fighting broke out six months ago and had lost his legs to a bomb dropped by an Indian plane.

"Professor Mathur, Professor Singh informs me that you are the expert on regeneration. My grandfather has said many fine things about your Institute; he suggested that I come here seeking aid."

Dave and Shashi exchanged looks. There had been nothing casual about dropping Sri Karji's name. If they succeeded in restoring Husain's legs, the sky would be the limit for future research; but if they failed . . .

"I'm sorry, Sri Husain, but there is nothing we can do for you. Our efforts here are aimed primarily at overcoming the worldwide drop in birth rate following the Cataclysm. Only a few of us, like Dr. Singh and myself, are pursuing lines of research in other areas of biology, and primary regeneration is not one of them."

"But Dr. Singh said that you were working on regeneration."

"Yes and no. Let me explain. We have had some success with primary regeneration where the matrix of tissue was not entirely destroyed. Consider the amputation of an arm—say, between the elbow and the wrist. We could cause all of the muscles of the forearm to regenerate and replace the bone with metal. But the hand? The fingers? There would be no matrix for their regeneration. In certain cases of limited avulsion we use this technique, but it means nothing to you.

"Furthermore, we have isolated hormones that cause 'stunted growth', so that we can give treatment to a child whose limbs do not fully develop; but full, primary regeneration in living humans is impossible, at least within the foreseeable future. It has to take place at the embryonic stage."

Husain's expression hardened, as if he were unwilling to believe.

"What I am doing is experimenting with the growth of replacement parts from clones."

"Clones?"

Shashi smiled. "Except for sperm and ova, every cell contains the genetic pattern of the entire organism. Certain lower orders—sponges, for example—reproduce by budding off of ordinary cells. The new organisms produced are genetically identical to the parent organism. We can artificially stimulate ordinary muscle cells to replicate new organisms in a similar way among the higher orders.

"For example, we take cells from a donor rat, clone them, and grow a new rat identical in every sense to the original. Whole limbs from the clone can then be transplanted surgically to the original."

"Can you do that with humans?"

"No, not yet, nor any time in the reasonably near future. The problems involved are staggering."

"Nor are all the problems scientific," Dave pointed out. "Consider the rats. They are in every way identical; if they were human, what right would a man have to steal a part from his clone?"

"Also," Shashi went on, "if that were not a problem, consider that to produce a clone with a body of your present age would require about twenty years of growth, by which time you would be forty. In order to be practical, clone replacements would have to begin their growth at the time of the subject's birth."

"Have human clones been raised?"

Shashi nodded. "In China before the Cataclysm there were reported to have been human clones raised by implantation *in uteri*. It is even told that a clone of Chairman Mao was raised, but that story is probably apocryphal. Since the Cataclysm, experiments with clones have been common. There are at present at least a hundred clone-conceived persons in India alone, some of whom are nearly thirty years old."

Husain was shocked. "I had no idea!"

"It isn't exactly top secret, but it is not yet publicized.

We think that it may be a stopgap measure for the next several generations until we solve the birth rate problem."

"Then you could make a clone from my cells?"

"Yes, but if we did it would merely provide you with a son, not a new set of legs; and that son would look and be no different from any other child, except that he would be your genetic twin. He might not even resemble you that closely as he grows; environment has its effect, too."

Dave turned to Shashi after Husain had left. "You lied to him pretty badly."

"You mean Choudry's forced growth enzyme? Why should I get his hopes up over an untried technique? Anyway, forced growth doesn't overcome the moral problems."

Dave stared at the door where Husain had exited. "Perhaps."

Shashi stared at him, disturbed by the implications of his speculation.

Chapter 3

IT HUNG IN A VOID WHERE THERE WAS no sound, no light, no change of temperature and no gravity. It had hung thus since its birth, so that it knew nothing. Physically, it existed; mentally, it had never left the womb.

An umbilical cord brought it air and sustenance, and the enzymes that forced its growth. And that growth was phenomenal—three weeks from birth to physical maturity.

Dave turned away from the meters on the sensory deprivation tank and checked the readings on the computer. In a second tank, a bottle-nosed dolphin called Baba lay half in and half out of the water, narcotized and attached to an umbilical similar to the one on the sensory deprivation tank. Dave made final checks all around and fed a narcotic to the already mindless dolphin within the sensory deprivation tank; it was needless now but would help that one's transition to sentient life.

He closed a switch. There was a hum as new banks of machinery came into play, but the moment was largely

31

unremarkable. The machinery stripped the dolphin Baba of every hint of memory, and, in the process, the dolphin died.

Dave confirmed that fact, then opened the sensory deprivation tank. For the first time, light impinged upon the dolphin called Baba II, but it did not react because of the narcotic he had given it.

Dave was playing games with Baba II when Shashi came in later that afternoon. He frolicked about the larger tank, entirely unaware that he had, in one sense, been living only a few hours.

Dave greeted Shashi as she touched his hand and leaned down to stroke the dolphin's head. Then she froze in mid-gesture, staring at it; the tattoo that had identified the creature no longer adorned its forehead. Jerking back, she looked sideways at him in a mixture of wariness and shocked admiration. "You did it!"

"Yes."

"And Baba is . . . dead?"

He shook his head. "Transmigrated. Baba's memories reside now in the brain of Baba II. Baba II is Baba, brain and bone."

Shashi watched in wonder as the creature shot about the tank. She herself had cultured the clone that now swam before her, and she had assisted Dave in the surgery which had implanted the fetus in a dolphin host mother. Raised from birth in a sensory deprivation tank, it had had no memories and no personality of its own until now.

"Baba—the original Baba—is dead?"

Dave nodded, unconcerned, then said, "Watch." For twenty minutes he put Baba II through his paces, and he responded beautifully, threading the intricate maze of wires and mirrors with its innumerable turnings and false leads. Dave had spent months training Baba in that maze and it was one that no creature, however intelligent, could have traversed without error except from prior experience. But Baba's memories now resided in Baba II, and since Baba II's body was a clone from Baba, it was identical in every genetic particular. By heredity and environment, Baba II *was* Baba, differing only in the slight pallor of II's skin and his lack of Baba's identifying tattoo.

After his run through the maze, Baba II came for his reward of fish and remained to be fondled. As Shashi scratched him in all his favorite places, she realized that the situation would have been uncanny, except that the illusion that this was the original Baba was so convincing that she could not react emotionally to the situation.

They left the laboratory at sunset, walking past the open stalls of Poona, buying *chappatis* and tea in an insulated container, and went on up to the park. There they sat quietly until the sky faded and those few stars which could compete with the city lights came out. The air was chill, and Shashi drew close to Dave; yet she seemed somehow restrained.

"What's wrong?"

"Baba. I am deeply troubled by the implications of your experiment with him."

"I didn't kill Baba. I know you were fond of him; so was—am—I, but he is as alive tonight as he was this morning. Only his address has changed."

The faint attempt at humor failed. "I didn't mean that. I know I made a pet of him, but if he had to die, I wouldn't cry. I said that I am troubled by the implications, not the actuality, of what you have done."

"Meaning?"

"Meaning what happened to Baba's *atman?*"

"You don't really believe in that crap?"

"Yes."

There was little he could say in the face of such calm assertion, so he swallowed his irritation. "That which made Baba Baba was transferred from one body to the next. His *atman,* if you want to use that term, is what was transferred."

"No, Dave. You know better than that. His soul,

perhaps; you are the expert on Christian theology, not me. But not his *atman*.

"I know that I led many previous lives, but do I remember them? No. The *atman* which is my essence, which goes with me from life to life, is not memory."

Dave shrugged, unwilling to argue theology. His knowledge of Hinduism was considerable, but he could never hope to debate it with a native. Or a believer. It irritated him to think that Shashi could cling to what seemed to him to be superstitions; more important, those beliefs might hamper his work. And that work was a matter of life and death.

"What will you do next?"

"With Baba, nothing. Since we are not yet at a clinical stage, it would prove nothing to repeat the tranference to still another body. What I have to do next is choose a short-lived but fairly intelligent creature and do a transference from an aged individual into a young clone."

"In search of immortality?"

"Yes," he replied tightly. "I also have to follow up some leads on sensory-deprived clones as donors for organ transplants."

A troubled look crossed her face in the dim moonlight. He turned to her. "You are thinking of Husain?" She nodded. "Forget it," he said. "By the time we get our techniques ironed out, Husain will be an old man."

"I know."

He moved closer. She had changed from lab coveralls to a sari, and it did little to resist his motions in the sweet darkness.

Shashi Mathur had been married at twelve, consummated at fourteen, and had lived with her husband, a man of thirty-five, until she was sixteen. At that point she had turned her sexual attentions elsewhere, trying to let no fertile night pass without a bedmate, preferably a new one each month. In that she was merely following the customs of the time. When births are rare, they are precious, and who can say what lucky coupling might prove fertile?

When Shashi was seventeen, her husband died. By that time she was convinced that she was barren. In that she was merely ordinary. Faced with the prospect of an empty future, she took her meager inheritance, left for Bombay, and enrolled in one of the dozen prep schools that surround Deccan University. Now she was twenty-four, certain of her barrenness, and working religiously to overcome that bane for her fellows.

As a professor, a widow, and a *kshatriya*, she enjoyed high status and a rare freedom from constricting gossip. Her quarters were furnished with utmost simplicity. She had a small brazier where she kindled a charcoal fire on those nights when the monsoon drove chill and dampness through the walls and windows. She often brewed tea there for herself or her guests, but never cooked. There were stalls of sweet-wallas within a five-minute walk, and she ate her main meals at the Institute cafeteria.

Her single room was unfurnished, save for cushions and a foam sleeping pad. By day this was propped against a bare inner wall. Block-printed Madrasi hangings adorned the walls and thick rush mats covered the floor. A carved chest held her clothing. There was a row of books against one wall: the *Gita*, Vivekananda's works, Tagore's poetry, and the like. She kept her professional books strictly segregated in her office at the Institute.

By the light of candles, with incense sticks burning, she lit the brazier and did oblations to Agni. Then she settled into the lotus position.

Later, after her meditations, after she had extinguished the lights, her mind strayed back to Ram Singh, a name she preferred to the ridiculous "Dave", and his unnatural playing with the structure of reality.

The summons came at noon the following day. "Sri Singhji?" The messenger bowed from the waist and

Dave felt an irrational irritation at his obeisance. Messages proffered with the double honorific, prefix and suffix, usually meant trouble. It read:

> Sri Kantikar of Bombay would appreciate your presence at his bungalow on Tagore Street at eight P.M. on the night of the twenty-fifth to discuss a matter of mutual interest.
>
> J. K.

For a moment Dave was too stunned to take in all the implications of the words. So the Premier wanted to see him personally; and unofficially, to judge from the fact that he signed the message without reference to his office and had set the meeting in his own house. Dave had neither met nor had any dealings with Sri Karji; had never seen him except for newcasts. It could only concern his grandson.

Dave had known that Husain had not dropped his grandfather's name casually. Cold sweat popped out on his face as he studied the note.

Chapter 4

BOMBAY WAS THE WORLD'S MOST MODern city, in the best and worst senses of the word. The capital of India since Dehli's inundation, it housed an impressive neo-Ashokan capitol complex surrounded by a buffer and expansion zone of parks. Beyond that, the city was aggressively utilitarian.

Even as early as the Cataclysm, India had been short of construction timber, though it supplied much of the world's decorative hardwoods. Adobe, rammed earth, and stone had been her building materials for centuries, and still were, but with a difference. Adobe bricks were made in huge factories, chemically stabilized and force-dried. Rammed-earth walls were also chemically stabilized and made now by special hydraulic rams and molds. Human labor was no longer a cheap commodity and, with declining population, would become more scarce as time passed, but electricity was plentiful from fusion reactors.

Stone had been a major building material, but it, too, required massive inputs of human labor to quarry and lay. Now stone was quarried mechanically as gravel and fused into monolithic blocks *in situ* at a tremendous cost of power. All public buildings were constructed of this magmastone, as were dams, the houses of the rich, public monuments, and, of course, the great dykes of the Ganga and Panch-ab projects.

Dave debarked at Tagore station, skirted the power plant, and strode toward Kulin Hill. His route took him through the Avenue of Abominations, where beggars from the whole of Maharashtra gathered. Some were normal enough, a few were amputees and other accident or disease victims, but by far the majority were mutants. Unable to compete with their normal fellows and of execrable status (Sri Karji called them the "new untouchables" and begged Congress to pass laws protecting them, all to no avail), they were reduced to living on public pity. One was eyeless with an unbroken expanse of skin rising from his rudimentary nose up to his hairline, another had a shriveled third arm projecting like a grotesque *lingam* from between her breasts, another . . . They cried out to him as he passed, their arms waving up from their lotus positions like anemones.

Kulin Hill rose like a tower of sanity. From its summit the city took on a certain geometric beauty as distance hid her less graceful aspects. The summit was surrounded by a ten-meter-high magmastone wall, pierced infrequently by small gates, and only the onion-domed turret which would serve its residents as an observation post was visible from the ground outside. Out in the harbor, ships were switching on their lights, while beneath them, lost in the cold, wet darkness of the sea bottom, Old Bombay lay. One could take an excursion submarine to visit the ruins, but Dave found the idea a little depressing.

The house within the wall was a disappointment. It was a faithful rendition of Indian architecture, but in magmastone and bitudobe it simply did not have the grace of Arjuna or Chitradurga. Of all the cities in India, Bombay was the least Indian; everything was a modern copy of past glories, and thus lacked both the charm of the old and the boldness of the new. Even Poona, the Mecca of the modern Indian, still retained its old quarter.

He was led through the cavernous mansion and up the winding, open stairway to the observation tower. Here, beneath the dome in a glass-walled room whose clear panels had been thrown open to admit the night air, sat Sri Karji. He was lounging in a rattan peacock chair, surrounded by a scattering of manila-bound reports. A tea service sat on a cart nearby and he responded to Dave's *namaste* by waving him to a chair opposite him. A servant materialized to serve the tea and chutneys as Sri Karji studied him impassively, withholding conversation until they were alone. Somewhere within the house, a sitarist was playing *Raga Rageshri,* an evening raga.

"It was good of you to come, Sri Singhji."

"It was good of you to ask me."

"How have you liked India?"

Dave put on a smile he didn't feel. "Really, one does not ask that question of a native. I am a citizen, you know."

"Yes. Since last October, was it not?"

Dave nodded, having no doubt that Kantikar knew the exact date and anything else he felt would be useful. It was some relief to be a citizen of the Indian Commonwealth; at least he could not be deported. Shot, but not deported.

"We have a number of scientists from other countries working in our universities. They bring a welcome change of orientation that often bears well on our problems. One should always try to maintain a fresh viewpoint.

"Many of our visiting scientists eventually ask for asylum, especially those from Africa and the Andean Republic, and we never turn them away. However, we do not normally grant them citizenship, for political reasons."

"Of course."

"You present a new situation. We have not found training in NorAm to be adequate, so I was surprised to find that one of our top scientists at the Institute was a North American."

"I took my graduate training at Deccan."

"So I discovered. You have risen high."

Condescension disguised as praise. The civilized man speaking to the barbarian. What you really mean, old man, is that I am vulnerable. Dave shrugged deprecatingly.

"I understand that you met my grandson?"

"Yes. A sad case; perhaps in twenty years medicine can help him."

Kantikar changed the subject abruptly. "I understand that you are an agnostic—so it said on your application for citizenship. Yet, were you not raised as a Pentecostal-Baptist?"

Despite himself, Dave gave grudging respect for the man's unabashed highhandedness. As Premier, his power was virtually limitless, and he apparently saw no advantage in hiding it, save behind a thin facade of politeness. "A Millennialist," Dave replied. "There are minor doctrinal differences between the two."

"But you cast all that aside?"

"Yes, when I was fifteen."

"So I surmised after reading your article in the *Deccan Monitor.*"

"I hope you don't rely on that article as an index of my sophistication. I wrote it for the school paper my first year at Deccan and my command of NaiHind was anything but complete."

Kantikar waved the protest aside. "The sense of your arguments came through despite any inadequacies of language. You believe that both the Christian concept of soul and the Hindu concept of *atman* are in error."

"Yes."

"And that the only thing that exists is biological

drives tied to experience—'tied by cords of memory' was your felicitous phrase, I believe."

"Yes."

"An old idea—not that you claimed it was not. But you carried it further by saying that if a man's biology could be replicated by parthenogenesis—cloning—and his memory transcribed, he could attain virtual immortality."

Tired of playing parrot, Dave said nothing.

"Once again, not a new idea. Yet you go on to say that man's religions have cheated him out of immortality by making him accept the idea of death; that these techniques of 'physiological resurrection' would have been perfected centuries ago if men really believed in their own mortality."

Kantikar paused with a show of expectation, but Dave simply shrugged. "You seem well versed in what I wrote. I see no reason to enlarge upon it."

"Such a philosophy must make a man quite desperate. To think that immortality is at hand but that he might not be able to perfect its techniques before he dies—I do not envy you."

It was some hours later that the conversation turned serious again. All through dinner, Kantikar had refused to be drawn into any but the most trivial discussions, and later he had been intent on the musicians and the Kathak dancers. Finally, as they sat back in rattan lounges on the terrace watching the moon on Bombay harbor and listening to the distant sound of Kantikar's resident sitarist playing in the courtyard below, each with a small water pipe of *gunga* spreading its mild narcotic through their systems, Kantikar returned to the discussion.

"Dr. Mathur told my grandson that one reason she could not provide replacement limbs was that it would take twenty years to grow them. Yet my aides have discovered an article by Professor Choudry of your

Institute that indicates that clone growth can be forced to many times normal speed."

Dave was cautious in his reply. "We have had some success along those lines with laboratory animals."

"And human clones?"

"We have not tried it with human clones."

"Yet if you tried it, and failed, what harm would be done? The human from whom the clone cells were taken would be entirely unaffected."

"True. But we aren't sure whether or not a limb so forced would adversely affect the original donor after the transplant. Also, there is the moral aspect."

"That should prove no problem for you."

"Sir?"

Kantikar paused, looking up at the moon, then went on: "It is your philosophy, avowed in the article we discussed earlier, that memory is the only 'soul' a man has. A clone grown to maturity in a sensory deprivation tank would have no memory and could be used as a donor with as complete immunity from moral censure as a cadaver. That is your philosophy, is it not?"

Dave felt the trap closing; yet he did not regret it. It was a step that had to be taken eventually, and if Kantikar ordered it, the blame would be his if public opinion turned against them.

"By the way, how is Baba II doing?"

Dave actually grinned. "Well." Then he added, "There is no guarantee that Baba II will not die tomorrow from some unforeseen complication, and that goes even more strongly for Husain."

"At this preliminary stage, we need not worry about that. When the time comes to take risks, we will all review the situation together and decide what is best."

"Will you send him by tomorrow?"

"You want to get a clone started? Very well, but he can only stay an hour. He is leaving for Medina on a mission of utmost delicacy."

Dave was suddenly aware of greater depths of machination than he had suspected before. "You aren't just the doting grandfather, are you? You want to show the Muslims that they can be outdone. Nirghaz's crippling by Indian bombs was a major diplomatic blunder, wasn't it?"

Kantikar's eyes were cold. "That, Singhji, is none of your business."

Chapter 5

HUSAIN DEPOSITED A CELL SAMPLE which Shashi cultured for cloning. Growing a human clone was not greatly different from growing an animal clone, and the apparatus of a mechanical womb could be set up quickly, but the sensory deprivation tank was another matter. It had to be larger and more sophisticated, but such tanks had been built before. It was a job requiring no new technology.

During the first five weeks of gestation, no growth stimulants were used, but by that time a completion date for the S.D. tank was reasonably certain and the Choudry enzymes were released into the fluid where the embryo floated. A month later it had reached four kilos, and Dave, with Shashi's aid, transferred the infant to the tank that had held Baba II, carefully severing the fleshy umbilical and replacing it with a mechanical one which fitted the orifices of the head.

"Quite well," Dave replied to Husain's query. "Couldn't be better, in fact. The clone is in the sensory deprivation tank that housed one of our test animals and will remain there until the larger tank is built. We aren't pushing its growth as much as we might because we don't want it to outgrow its present home before a new one is finished."

Nirghaz Husain bobbed his head in tense delight. It was obvious that he was only now allowing himself to hope. He had returned from Medina yesterday after long and fruitless negotiations with the Muslims. Dave wheeled him into an examination room and said, "Nirghaz, this is Dr. Choudry. In addition to being the one who developed the growth stimulant, he is also an accomplished surgeon, which neither Dr. Mathur nor I is."

Dave and Choudry each took an arm and hoisted Husain onto the examining table, where Shashi unbuttoned his gown with asexual efficiency.

Dave drew a breath and held himself very still. He had no bedside manner to cover this situation. Shashi turned away, but Choudry went on with admirable calm. "You didn't inform us that your genitalia had also been lost."

"Amputated. Like the legs, they were too crushed to save." Husain looked away, but his eyes were hard and bitter. "So they said."

"Hmm."

Without looking at them, Husain asked, "Is there any chance of transplanting that, too?"

"Dammit, man, don't spring a question like that on me out of thin air! I don't know."

His belly and buttocks were a webwork of scar tissue and his body terminated in a blank and lumpy mass. Choudry probed and measured, then sent Husain away for X rays.

In the dimly lighted office, Choudry had taped a dozen X rays taken from all angles on a battery of viewing boxes. He sat hunched over one, overlay paper and ruler in his hand, measuring, checking angles with an ordinary protractor, and occasionally pausing to calculate. He had been at it for better than an hour. Dave and Shashi had given up following the complexities of his work and were sitting hip to hip on a desktop across the room sharing coffee. It looked bad.

Finally, he laid his paraphernalia aside and stretched, then shook his head. "No way."

"I can't believe it," Dave said. "Here we were prepared to use the latest techniques, and even an entirely new donor source, and we can't proceed because our surgery isn't up to it!"

"Let me put it this way, Ram. If he were lying on the table now as a fresh amputee and we had the parts available, I would try it. We would have nothing to lose because he would have only a slim chance of living, either way.

"I frankly don't know how he lived. You can be sure that the abdominal cavity was wide open; they certainly had to push his viscera back as they sutured."

Shashi shook her head. "Why did they go to such lengths for an Indian?"

"Politics!" Dave fairly snarled. "The fact that Nirghaz was injured by Indian bombs was a diplomatic coup for the Medinans. Had he died, it would have soon been forgotten, but now he is a walking—I mean a *living*—monument to Indian aggression."

"All of which doesn't help him or us," Choudry went on. "Look at this. The left articular fossa is completely gone and the ilium has been trimmed. The head of the right femur is still in place and fused into the fossa. Any transplant would have to begin above that point and include the entire pelvic girdle. Surgery just isn't up to it."

"So who tells him?"

Dave did not go directly to speak with Nirghaz; instead, he went to his lab, where Baba II greeted him with insistent snortings which stopped only when Dave scratched his head and tossed him a chunk of fish.

Science, Dave knew, proceeds by fits and starts, not

so much because research is quixotic (though it is), but because a man can invent or discover only what mankind is ready for. Leonardo da Vinci's model helicopters were proof of that.

Had the time come? It was a delicate question concerning not so much the state of the art as the spirit of the times. He had Sri Karji's support. There was money and power there, and in this state of near war, the label of "military secret" would instantly hide Dave's activities from the public.

But not from his colleagues. He still had not convinced Shashi of the inhumanity of a sensory-deprived clone, and Choudry had been hesitant. Would they have balked at cutting up a seemingly live and healthy human like some test animal, despite the fact that it was "merely" a clone? He wasn't sure. It loomed as a large possibility that he would never have gotten away with the transplant even if medical reasons had not intervened.

Or had they? Had Choudry deliberately misread the X rays? No matter; either way, this new course of action was better for both Dave and Husain. And humanity.

He went down to the waiting room. Nirghaz had given up the pretense of reading while he waited and looked up intently at Dave's entrance.

"Can it be done?"

Dave stared at Husain for a long time before answering. "No, not by surgery. But . . ."

Chapter 6

BABA II SHOT ACROSS THE TANK, UNDER a bar, through a ring, described a complex spiral around a horizontal rod, doubled back—and faltered. Confused, he floated free for a moment, then shot across the tank for a piece of fish and a scratch on the head.

Sri Karji straightened up and shook his head. "An impressive display, I suppose, if I knew what it meant."

Dave slapped the dolphin and turned back to Kantikar. "That is just the problem. You impressed me so much in our first interview that I assumed your spies had been thorough. They were not, or you would know that what you just witnessed is the reason we have to have the Deliac computer. Your spies told you, correctly, that Baba II could thread a complex maze using the original Baba's memories. What they did not tell you was that we trained Baba in five separate mazes. Baba II can do three of them perfectly, one not at all, and the other partway before faltering."

"So your experiment was not a perfect success, as you said it was."

"*You* told *me* that my experiment had succeeded, not vice versa. And I assumed that your information was complete.

"In fact, the experiment succeeded admirably, and we know why it failed and the exact dimensions of our failure. We took every memory that Baba could give in one burst of energy before it killed him. Had we taken the memories in increments and stored them in a computer bank, we could have gotten them all.

"But we didn't have such a computer because of budgetary limitations. When you gave me the commission of rejuvenating Nirghaz, I assumed that you knew that the computer was necessary."

Kantikar stared unseeing down at the frolicking dolphin. It was always galling to be outdone by a competitor; to be caught up by one's own failings was doubly humiliating. Worse, it made all his efforts to date useless unless he came through on this latest demand. Of course, it could be done. Anything, legal or illegal, could be done. But every such action left him open to attack, and there were always those who were ready to pull down Sri Karji.

Nor should he divert even a fraction of his country's energies from the upcoming struggle for survival. The Deliac computer was an auxiliary setup in the Deliac Air Force complex south of Poona. It was presently not being used, but it might be needed on short notice.

Yet there was a debt to pay; there was his affection and there was his guilt. For it was Sri Karji who had ordered the airstrikes against Mahmet, knowing full well that his grandson was there, but confident in the odds that he would emerge unhurt. It had meant surprise and it had given him a reputation for putting the good of the state above his personal welfare. But the price . . . It was one thing to calculate chances beforehand and quite another to find oneself the loser afterward.

Nor had the airstrikes ended the Medinan menace; if anything, it had stiffened resistance.

It was bad enough that Nirghaz must regain his legs in a way so unorthodox that it smacked of heresy. Transplants were one thing; the transference of memory was quite another. Still, if Nirghaz were willing, how could Kantikar hold back? "I'll give the orders."

After Kantikar and his entourage had left, Shashi found Dave leaning on the edge of the dolphin tank, his face lined and worried. As always, she was both drawn to and troubled by his iron control, so different from other men she had known. Even other NorAm men had not been like this. She had a brief vision of a creature trapped inside a drum of steel, crying out for attention, for understanding. What was that creature like? After two years of liaison with Ram David, she still could not truly say.

"Did you pull it off?"

Dave nodded, then shook his head. He staggered as he moved across the room to drop into his favorite chair. She realized that he was emotionally exhausted. "Shashi, if he ever finds out how I lied to him, I just don't know what he'll do."

She patted his arm. "It wasn't your fault."

"The hell it wasn't. I should have put Baba II through his paces immediately, but I was too exultant over my apparent success. Then came Kantikar's summons and the work with his grandson. I let basic caution slip."

"He doesn't know that."

"No, not now, but I'll always wonder when he might find out. If I pull this off, it will get me off the hook, but otherwise . . ."

"*I?* I thought this was a team effort."

"You know what I meant."

"Yes. I know that you meant exactly what you said.

This is your holy grail. You are working your way to heaven. First transfer Nirghaz into a new body, then clone a standby for yourself. And when you feel old age and death whispering at your neck, you'll run and hide in your fine, new, *young* body."

"Well, what's wrong with that?"

She merely shook her head and said, *"Maya."*

"Sometimes you sound like a guru. This world is no illusion. Rebirth is the illusion."

"You say—but you have no proof that it is so."

"Nor have you."

"True," she said, unperturbed. "One does not look to illusion for proof of illusion's nonexistence."

They stared at one another, each caught up in his own neat, circular pattern of argument. Then she slid by the issue by settling in against his knee and taking his hand. "Ram."

He smiled and let some of the tension drain away. "Yes, love?"

"About my barrenness." He started, for barrenness was a subject of deep taboo which no barren woman would willingly discuss. "My ova are infertile, but I am anatomically normal."

She paused for a very long time then. He did not know what she was driving at; he already knew that she could carry an embryo to term if artificially implanted, but there were tens of thousands of women who would willingly do that if fertile ova were available. "Ram Singh, my lover, will you give me your child? Your clonechild."

He was stunned. "Wouldn't you rather the child be of your own heritage?"

She shook her head. "Yours, love; yours." He looked down at her tense face and was deeply moved. He nodded and she came into his lap, kissing him and crying.

His fingers touched the bandage on his forearm where the tissue had been taken, reflecting on the reversed symbolism of that wound. Across the room, Shashi worked deftly, lovingly, culturing the cells for cloning. It took her three hours. Sunlight slanted in from the west across the lab (so orderly in contrast to his) as she finished, still humming the tune with which she had filled up the afternoon.

He took her hand casually when she had finished, but she pulled his face down for a kiss that was anything but casual. He held her close, thinking that he had never seen her more beautiful. "Tomorrow," she said, "I'll get Dr. Choudry to do the implant."

"Are you sure this is what you want?" She nodded and smiled still more deeply.

"Tonight, we celebrate."

"How do you celebrate the initiation of a pregnancy?" he asked, deadpan, and she giggled outright.

That night he moved into Shashi's quarters. They were crowded, but it didn't matter. Neither of them gave much time to sleeping then.

Whether it was his near brush with Sri Karji's wrath or Shashi's commitment to him, he could not have said, but the urgency of his quest for immortality came back to him renewed. The next morning he sent a letter to an old friend and professor in NorAm, James Brigham, whose accomplishments he had long since outstripped but whose wisdom he respected. That letter contained an outline of what he had done and the promise of detailed explanations to be forthcoming. He also instructed Brigham to prepare to publish his notes in the event of his death, feeling that once enough people knew of the resurrection process, nothing could stop mankind from rising up to demand its universal implementation.

Chapter 7

NIRGHAZ HAD NOT ENJOYED HIS FIRST interview with Colonel Mohan Bhatt, Commandant of the Deliac base. Bhatt was the nephew of Gopal Bhargava, the opposition leader, which made such semi-legal circumventions as Sri Karji was engaging in ticklish. Whatever happened on Deliac base would be reported immediately to Bhargava.

Well, no matter. Kantikar had slapped a net of security around the small section of the base that Singh's project was to occupy that not even Bhatt could penetrate. Normally, Nirghaz would question the wisdom of antagonizing a base commander, but Bhatt was so firmly in the enemy camp that no harm would be done.

Nirghaz left Deliac base and traveled southward toward Bangalore, but turned off on a barely maintained side road after going only a few kilometers. He followed the rutted track carefully, for he had had little experience in piloting a monopod himself since his accident. It was a simple enough vehicle, an LOX/LH powered fuel cell, an electric motor and a continuously variable automatic transmission. All the controls had been re-rigged so that Nirghaz could handle them.

He traveled a kilometer before he reached the checkpoint. Thereafter the road was better, no longer needing the camouflage of disrepair.

Not even Bhatt knew of the Nehru project; nor did Bhargava—supposedly. Nirghaz was not sure on that count; one could so seldom be sure of anything when security and political power were involved.

Kantikar was waiting for him when he had undergone the various delays and indignities involved in security checks. Nirghaz knew of the project but had not visited it before; indeed, Kantikar had been here only a few times. Those who worked past the fourth layer of guards had not left the project since its inception four years earlier; they were housed, fed, and entertained here beneath an unexceptional mountain deep in the Western Ghats.

Kantikar met him with a smile, returned his *namaste,* and touched him lightly on the shoulder. "General Ullah, this is my grandson and ambassador to Medina, Nirghaz Husain." Ullah greeted him with correct neutrality. "He is privy to all state secrets, without exception. He has known of the Nehru since its beginning—longer than you have, in fact."

"A pity we haven't had a chance to meet before," Ullah said.

"Thank you. As you know, my duties keep me quite busy."

"However," Kantikar cut in, "I am getting older every day, and the recent assassination attempt brought my mortality home to me in a very pointed fashion."

"A shameful thing," Ullah said. "Our security forces should have protected you better. I trust the persons responsible were punished."

"The assassin died on the spot and my former security chief is now an agricultural inspector in Tamilnad. As for the instigators of the assassination, you may be sure that they will be found out and punished appropriately."

Kantikar looked meaningfully at Ullah, but he only replied, "Yes, we will soon teach the Medinans a lesson."

Nirghaz knew that Kantikar was not convinced that the assassination had been ordered by Medina. He suspected that it had been engineered by Bhargava, and Ullah was of Bhargava's political camp. But without proof, Kantikar was powerless to move against them.

Ullah led the way deeper into the bunker, past shops and research complexes whose purposes Nirghaz could not guess. These were the auxiliary aspects of the base; they had been all important in the development of the Nehru and were still of prime importance in protecting it, but the heart of the base was the Nehru itself.

It was housed in a gigantic underground hangar, lighted on all sides by massive floods. An oblate spheroid nearly five hundred meters along its long axis, it represented the ultimate weapon available to India at that time, an orbital launching platform for fusion bomb missiles.

It took most of the day for them to work their way from the compact fusion reactor that would power the platform, through the endless corridors to the conning chamber at the heart of the vessel.

The Nehru carried a hundred darts, each a slim, winged vessel twenty meters long and three meters in diameter. Externally, they were identical, so that there could be no way for an enemy to tell whether a dart were manned or unmanned, armed with a warhead or with minirockets.

Ullah was like a proud father with his favorite child.

"We carry a crew of one hundred fifty: one third assigned to the Nehru itself, one third to the drone darts, and one third to the manned darts.

"The platform itself will hang in stationary orbit above the equator just halfway between Medina and India, but it will have the capacity to reposition itself at will. It will even be able to hover in a stationary quasi-orbit over any spot on the globe, at any height. This will not only make it a more strategic weapon, but will have a tremendous psychological effect."

"Something I don't understand," Nirghaz cut in, "is what advantage is gained by a stationary orbit. That will place this platform several times farther away from Medina than our land-based missiles."

"Inaccessibility to counterattack; at that height any missile will have to fight gravity to reach the Nehru, giving us time to take evasive action or to send out darts. Contrariwise, any missile launched downward will continue to accelerate all the way, becoming progressively more difficult to intercept."

"Then the Nehru is basically an offensive weapon."

"Nonsense!" Ullah snapped. "The differentiation between offense and defense is strictly artificial.

"The Nehru, you will note, needs no auxiliary rockets to launch her. The fusion pile will generate up to three gravities for a sustained period, more than enough to reach Mars or Venus without refueling, if that were her mission. This allows the Nehru to remain in space indefinitely."

Ullah led them back out and left them when Kantikar refused his invitation to dinner, claiming prior engagements. Nirghaz had said little throughout the day.

"What do you think?" Kantikar asked.

"It terrifies me."

"Me, too. I sometimes wish that I hadn't agreed to it; but then I realize that I had no choice. A man often does what he dislikes, because he has no choice."

Nirghaz shrugged, embarrassed by the veiled reference to the bombing of Mahmet. Kantikar continued: "The Medinans seem to have some idea that we are constructing an orbital platform. That seems a natural thing, after all—a reasonable next step in our escalating war. They have begun building one of their own."

Nirghaz had not heard, but he was not surprised. "What are we doing about it?"

"We identified one of their major informants in Congress about a month ago. I managed to leak to him partial data on the Nehru—not anything important, but enough to put some teeth in the negotiations. We can't let them know what we have, but we have to make them fear that it is powerful."

"And if they refuse to desist?"

Kantikar scowled. "Nirghaz, you have to get them to stop. If they don't, I'll have to order the Nehru launched. If I didn't, Bhargava would ask for a vote of confidence—and I would lose. You know what he would do if he were in power."

"Use the Nehru for everything it's worth."

"Right. He would cow the Medinans into immediate concessions—then in twenty years we would have it all to do over again with bigger weapons and bigger risks."

He stared out the window at the rapidly darkening landscape. "I would give almost anything to be free of this burden. It brings me no pleasure. I am an old man; I should be a *vanaprastha,* laying aside the things of the world and preparing for my inevitable end. But I dare not.

"Nirghaz, if it weren't for you, I would give up. Only your contacts as Parivar Husain's son give me any hope of getting even a provisional peace."

"Grandfather," Nirghaz asked, "how much of a hand did you have in Mother's marriage?"

But Kantikar only smiled and shook his head.

"Parivar was a good man—a poor Muslim, but a good man. As I am a poor Hindu." He paused for a while, then went on: "That's what scares me about Bhargava; he's a good Hindu. A man who believes too strongly in his religion always believes too strongly in himself."

Chapter 8

DAVE DROPPED INTO THE SPARSE GRASS and slipped out of the straps of his pack. He sipped from his canteen and rummaged for a sandwich. All morning he had shared the trail with a stream of pilgrims heading for the shrine at the spring on the hillside below, but he had gone on when they had stopped. They carried *ghee* and flowers to offer to the Siva *lingam*. Most of them were barren young women coming to petition the divine male essence for children.

He could see the shrine below him and the double line of women arriving and departing, but it was of little interest to him. He had lived in India long enough to transcend both fascination and disgust. Now all he felt watching them was the same dull anger that any religious activity stirred in him.

He lay back and stared at the sky. The leaves were thin and did little to shade him; he shifted so that the shadow of the tree trunk fell across his eyes. Tomorrow they would move to the Deliac Air Force complex and such walks as this would become less frequent, if not impossible.

The land around him was dry and hilly, both like and unlike the verdant Ozarks where he had been born. The memories they dredged up were an odd mixture of sadness and joy, most of the joy pre-dating his fifteenth year. That last year, sharing the cabin with his dying father after professing his agnosticism, was something that still did not bear remembering. The years before that were ignorant, impoverished, and hard, but not without their sweetness.

He dozed a little then, dreaming of hot, dusty, barefooted days and of the long summer afternoons sitting on a hillside like this one, overlooking the sea and wondering what the world beyond was like. Wondering at the same time what wonders and horrors lay in the forbidden city below. Well, he had found out, and life was good. Other than a residual bitterness toward all things godly, he felt at peace with nature and life.

But not with his fellowmen. Too much rested in the hands of others now. He had committed himself and Shashi to the resurrection project and had placed their fate in Kantikar's hands. He shivered to think what that might mean, but his driving need to conquer death forced him to accept the risk, for Shashi as well as for himself. At least it was likely that any repercussions would fall on him alone.

Thinking of Shashi always brought a smile, and today it brought the remembrance that she was undergoing the implant of his child. He had never expected her to so honor him. Would he, he wondered, have borne her clone child rather than his own had he been a woman? But if he were a woman, he would not be the person he was, so the question was nonsensical, as well as hypothetical, and he put it aside.

Shashi had sent a book with him, so he dug it out of his pack. It was a slim volume, selections from the last five centuries of Indian poetry. She had marked a page. It was *The Sunset of the Century,* by Rabindranath Tagore, written on the last day of the nineteenth

century. The Americans and Europeans had seen the
coming twentieth century as the culmination of human
progress, but the view from the East had been different. He read the poem slowly, then re-read the closing
lines.

Be not ashamed, my brothers, to stand before
    the proud and the powerful.
With your white robes of simpleness.
Let your crown be of humility, your freedom
    the freedom of the soul.
Build God's throne daily upon the ample bareness
    of your poverty.
And know that what is huge is not great and
    pride is not everlasting.

Dave rolled the lines around in his mind, seeing
Shashi in them. If only India would heed her own
ancient wisdom.

Two weeks later, at Deliac, Dave lay back sleepless
and stared at the ceiling. He had not yet accustomed
himself to sleeping in a sealed, air-conditioned cubicle,
and he still seethed inwardly at that damned lackey
lieutenant who had tried to block Shashi and him from
sharing quarters. What possible business of his was it,
anyway?

Shashi seemed to be equally ill at ease. She shifted
her weight again and he felt the firm pressure of her
thighs scissoring his leg and heard her steady, unsleeping breath in his ear.

The Deliac Air Force complex stretched across miles
of flat, sandy soil in a section of the Deccan south and
east of Poona, but a million miles removed in feeling
from that sanctuary of free inquiry. Dave had been met
by Colonel Bhatt and he had seemed willing enough to
attend to their needs, but there was no friendliness in
him. No doubt he had been told to cooperate and
would do so as long as it was necessary, but he had no

liking for top-secret projects to which he himself was not privy.

They were housed in a computer complex and in an adjacent, renovated hangar. Dave had spent a week supervising the placement of the equipment, including the all-important sensory deprivation tank with Husain's clone inside and the secondary tank he had ordered.

Shashi shifted her weight again and Dave sought out her hand. "Can't you sleep, either?" she asked.

"No. I've been thinking; after we tape and reconstruct Nirghaz, I think we may be able to persuade Kantikar to continue our funding and perhaps let us continue using the computer."

"Probably. I'm sure he will be very grateful."

"I intend to tape myself."

He listened for censure in her voice, but her reply was neutral. "I knew."

"I want to tape you, too."

A brief delay. "I knew that, too. I won't let you."

"Why?"

"I have no desire for rebirth—that way."

"Are you so content with a reincarnation that may not be anything but an illusion, and won't leave you your memories even if it is true?"

"Yes."

After a long, dark time of silent breathing, he said "Damn!"

She rolled over on her elbow and looked down at him in the dimness. "Ram, my lover and my love, you think only of the future; what of the past? Everything I am today—and everything you are, if you would just admit it—is the product of a hundred thousand previous incarnations. Every good thing I do, every kindness and every attention to my fellowman, is the good in me that is left after the purging effect of a thousand other lives. If I could live on forever, just twenty-four, just as happy in your love, it would be a kind of death. Never to change, never to be a child again, never to face truly new challenges, never to be reborn fresh and clean. What an awful fate. Death-in-life. That is what you offer."

"If you feel that way, why do you help me with Nirghaz?"

"Nirghaz is a special case. We aren't giving him immortality, just a new set of legs and genitalia."

"It could lead to immortality."

"Yes. But I will have no part in that."

"Then you won't let me tape you?"

"Never."

"And if I tape myself?"

She didn't answer at once, so he prompted: "Shashi, answer me."

"I think I may leave you."

"What?"

"I love you, Ramádav, but one lifetime is enough."

He turned away from her in anger and she did not try to call him back.

Chapter 9

NIRGHAZ LAY BACK, ENCASED IN THE temperature- and gravity-neutralizing fluid, his head encased in a helmet that cut off sound, sight, and smell. The salt water around him was exactly 98.6 degrees; the air that moved into his lungs held progressively less oxygen and a carefully balanced percentage of carbon dioxide. Respiration, metabolism, and cognition slowly lessened. There was no light, no taste, no touching, and, of sound, only the gentle susurration of incoming air.

Gradually, the sound of airflow changed to a pulsing whisper that lulled him still deeper into the trance, and the soft voice, Shashi's voice, that had always been there just below the level of his notice, spoke to him of sleep and of childhood; and his mind, cut free, remembered.

Light! As the sleep had been beyond sleep, so the awakening was violent beyond any awakening he had previously experienced. His disorientation changed to despair as the laughing, running child he had been in dreams became a legless horror once more. For a cold moment he was drowning in some gigantic, malign womb; then hands had him and lifted him into the chilly air of reality. He pawed the all-enveloping hood, but it was cleverly latched and he had to wait helplessly, fighting claustrophobia, while the lab assistants removed it.

He lay for a while dripping beneath the light blanket they had put over his naked body, watching with small interest as the assistants cleaned up the saline fluid from the floor and retired. Shashi came over with a smile to sit beside him and he reached out to take her hand, needing the touch of humanity to return him to the present. Ram David was hunched over a typeset, engaging in a dialog with the computer. His profile was frozen in a mask of utter concentration and there were no sounds in the room but those of human breathing, the humming respiration of machines, and the drip of salt water from the table where Nirghaz lay.

Nirghaz blinked back tears and Shashi dabbed his face. The memories dredged up were as fresh in his mind as if he had just lived them, not like those of a dream which vanish upon awakening: the desert outside Kabul; his mother's gentle beauty; his stern father returning home after another try at settling the dispute his Hindu wife and half-caste son had raised; the bougainvillaea vine outside his window down which he had climbed; the shouting, rock-throwing band of boys crying, "Hindu, Hindu, Hindu!"

Finally, Dave switched off his console and came to stand beside Shashi. Nirghaz felt an unexpected rush of black resentment for the legs he walked on and for his manhood. Dave and Shashi made no secret of their liaison. Jealousy burned bright inside Nirghaz and he fought it unsuccessfully, for it was not Shashi that he wanted, but his own lost manhood.

Dave smiled wearily. "We got it." Nirghaz nodded, too spent to feel elation. "You were under a trance much deeper than is ever used in therapy, so anything we missed is unlikely to be crucial."

"You didn't get it all?" Nirghaz felt an irrational fear growing within him. To gain a new body, but lose a part of *himself*—unthinkable.

"What did you do on the afternoon of the fourteenth of May the year you were four?"

Nirghaz hesitated, then shrugged. "I don't know."

"You went out with your father to pick up some chutneys for your mother and the taxi broke down on the way home. You were impressed by the way the driver repaired the trouble with a piece of wire and you learned a new obscenity listening to him."

Nirghaz still looked blank. "I don't remember."

Dave shook his head. "I didn't expect you to. It is unlikely that you will ever remember the incident, though you will, of course, remember us discussing it now. Yet you brought it up under trance. In short, once the transference is complete, you could undergo standard hypno-analysis and never show any gaps in your memory. Anything we did not get, you have forgotten completely."

Nirghaz looked relieved. Dave continued: "We are up to age five, but future sessions will not progress so rapidly. Your recall of incidents will increase according to some as-yet unknown exponent, so we will probably require thirty or forty sessions to get every memory on tape. The mind has an amazing capacity."

While Shashi went out for tea, Dave helped Nirghaz towel off and dress, then shifted him down into his wheelchair. When Shashi returned he had regained most of his composure and accepted the mild, warm stimulant gratefully. "Ramadav, one thing troubles me."

"What is that?"

"When you first acquainted me with the memory transference concept, it was a one-shot method. One's memory was transferred intact from an old or broken body into a new, healthy one. I could accept that; after all, it was not that different from our concept of transmigration. But this use of multiple taping sessions and a computer—well, look at it this way. When I was five years old my father took me out horseback riding for the first time. You have that on tape?" Dave nodded. "But I still remember it."

After a long pause, Dave prompted: "So?"

"So when you have all my memories on tape, I will still have them in my head. When you transcribe them into my new clone, I will still have my memories here in my head. *Which one will be me?*"

"The question won't arise," Dave assured him. "When we make the last tape and the transference, we will terminate life support to your previous body."

Nirghaz could only stare in shock. "You mean that there will really be two of me, and that you will kill one of them for the sake of a neat closure to the experiment!"

Dave fought back the desire to merely shrug. He had thought deeply along these lines, and had all of the legal and moral questions resolved to his own satisfaction. Still, he knew the evanescent nature of the questions and was not sure that he could win anyone over by the same arguments he had used to still his own doubts. Instead, he said, "It will be like going to sleep and waking up to find your body regenerated."

"No. That is no answer; if you did not kill me off, it would be like going to sleep and waking up to find someone with my memories and my rejuvenated body going on to live a separate life while I remain tied to this body."

"That won't happen."

Nirghaz shook his head. "It isn't good enough. Look, I am no orthodox Hindu. If I were, I would be looking for release from rebirth, not for a continuance of my life on earth. Yet I cannot simply follow your way. I *do* believe in an *atman,* an essence, and that essence cannot inhabit two places at once."

Dave ground his teeth. Shashi was sitting tensely,

watching them both. He knew that she agreed with Nirghaz. "Look, when you go to sleep, and then wake up, you don't consider yourself a different person simply because there is an eight-hour gap in your existence. It will be the same with the resurrection process."

"Maybe."

Shashi broke in. "Nirghaz, you are strictly a volunteer. If you don't want to go through with this, simply say so." Dave shot her a murderous look, which she chose to ignore.

"What other chance do I have?"

"There is the possibility of a brain transplant, but the prognosis on that would be very poor. Otherwise, you can simply go on as you are. You seem to have adapted well to your difficulties and you are no worse than many other cripples."

He almost snarled. Looking at Shashi's soft womanhood, he did not—could not—desire her, but he remembered what desire was, and desire's consummation. Burning with shame and loss, he said, "For now, let's continue, but I have to consider this very deeply before we conclude the experiments."

X-ray and ultraviolet sensors probed it continuously where visible light could never go and where infrared sensors would have been blinded by the uniformity of temperature. Electrical discharges shocked its muscles into motion from time to time so that they could grow. It had the appearance of a ten-year-old child, still floating fetal in the saline womb of the sensory deprivation chamber. Resemblance to Nirghaz at age ten was superficial at best, for this body had never run, twisted, played, or felt the darkening sun on its skin. Thin, flaccid, dead white, it floated obscene in the eternal night and slept mindlessly on.

Within Shashi's womb, unhurried by growth stimulants, a more natural fetus grew. It floated secure and ignorant of the unease that caused her to toss unsleeping on her pallet.

In another place, Nirghaz lay propped against a pile of cushions. He moved little and cautiously, for without legs he would tumble like an unspinning top if he were not careful. It was but one more indignity to add to all the others he bore daily. He read the *Milindapanha,* for Hinduism has always taken wisdom where it finds it, and Buddhism is in many ways but a variant of Hinduism. He read:

"You were once a baby lying on your back, tender and small and weak. Was that baby you, who are now grown up?"

"No, your Reverence, the baby was one being and I am another."

"If that is the case, your Majesty, you had no mother or father, and no teachers in learning, manners, or wisdom. . . . Is the boy who goes to school one being and the young man who has finished his education another? Does one person commit a crime and another suffer mutilation for it?"

"Of course not, your Reverence! But what do you say on the question?"

"I am the being I was when I was a baby," said the Elder . . . "for through the continuity of the body all stages of life are included in a pragmatic unity."

"Give me an illustration."

"Suppose a man were to light a lamp; would it burn all through the night?"

"Yes, it might."

"Now is the flame which burns in the middle watch the same as that which burned in the first?"

"No, your Reverence."

"Or is that which burns in the last watch the same as that which burned in the middle?"

"No, your Reverence."

"So there is one lamp in the first watch, another in the middle, and yet another in the last?"

"No. The same lamp gives light all through the night."

"Similarly, your Majesty, the continuity of phenomena is kept up. One person comes into existence, another passes away, and the sequence runs continuously without self-conscious existence, neither the same nor yet another."

Nirghaz sighed and laid the text aside, as troubled and confused as ever.

Chapter 10

Dr. James Brigham
Dept. of Biology, Roanoke University
Roanoke, Appalachia, NorAm

Dear Jim,

The political situation here continues to worsen, as you are no doubt aware. I fear that it may interfere with my work, but even more I fear that Nirghaz Husain may back out at the last minute. I had hoped that working in India, where the people have a conception of transmigration on which to hang the resurrection project, I would not have to contend with the same innate conservatism that I would have faced in NorAm. Damn all religions. They give the contentment of lies and hold mankind back from making their vague promises of heaven a true reality.

I find that *atman* is as insidious as *soul* ever was. Not that I really blame Husain for his reticence. I find it harder myself to accept the possibility of multiple, co-equal individuals that it was simply to accept transference. But the alternative is death, and death is no alternative.

However, if you don't really believe in death . . . you see my problem.

James, my old friend, I have given much thought to the ultimate implications of the resurrection process and it occurs to me that I am simply incapable, by temperament and training, of visualizing the incredible changes it will eventually bring about. My aims are so simple, so basic— immortality for myself. Dare I confess it? There has never been any motivation for my work but pure, selfish fear of death. Yet now I realize that I may not live to complete the work. You must have guessed that; you always were sensitive to others. Wisdom was never one of my attributes, but I know myself well enough to know that intelligence is no substitute for wisdom. That is why I write you these letters; that and the fear—growing daily— that you will have to publish my notes eventually in order to see that the work is not lost. Be careful! Do not let the notes fall into other hands than yours.

I am rambling. It is past midnight now and I am very tired. Husain had another taping session today and left in a foul and depressed mood. If he turns back from the experiments now, we will lose *years!* At best, Kantikar will cut us back to our previous level of support, and I fear that he might become angry with us and cut us off altogether. The man's power is frightening, and grows in direct proportion to the imminence of war. And, of course, we may all die in a nuclear fireball before you even see this letter. I shall try to send you updates twice weekly from now on, in case that occurs.

If it seems strange that one who has admitted selfishness as his only motivation should be so concerned with the welfare of the world at large, and that he should be so concerned to see that his work should outlive him . . . well, frankly, I find it strange myself. No amount of self-analysis seems to account for it, so I merely commend it to you for study. You often understood me better than I understood myself, anyway.

Enough misery. Shashi is well and her pregnancy proceeds without complication. Birth is due in seven months. I wish that you could meet her. And, no, we will not marry. That is her decision, but you should understand that as a Hindu widow, remarriage can only diminish her status. It is unlikely that we will be able to leave here until the Husain thing is decided one way or another, and I cannot advise you to come to India while war is imminent. Until we meet again, know that you have been a true friend.

Dave Singer

Dave sealed the letter and laid it aside. He stretched and walked across the lab to the coffeepot, drew a cup, and grimaced in distaste. The brew was thick, black, and awful, but he watered it down and drank it, anyway. It was past midnight and his head felt enlarged; his eyes were red and hot. Shashi would be long since asleep. Outside the lab he had heard nothing for hours but the passing of the sentry. There had been guards ever since they moved to the Deliac complex. Nirghaz Husain had had the use of a sensory deprivation tank and a battery of onlooking technicians. Dave had only himself. He settled the cap atop his head and made sure that the electrodes pierced the appropriate points on his scalp. It was only one more small irritation to add to his sleeplessness. He felt light-headed as he settled back. He drew a syringe of amber fluid and found a vein. Then he began to recite, *"Om mani padme um . . ."*

Terminating its run, the computer sent a preemptory jolt of electricity through the scalp electrodes, shocking

Dave instantly awake. He tore off the cap, tears streaming down his face as the memory of his long-dead mother faded. For five hours he had been a child again, and there was no one to ease his transition back to reality.

He staggered as he crossed the lab. The computer chuckled, burped, and hummed its mechanical contentment. If only the throbbing in his head would stop.

It took another hour to recover the first of his lifetapes and to instruct the computer to forget the night's work. Then he staggered out to greet the sunrise.

In the weeks that followed, Dave continued his nightly tapings and each morning he forwarded the new lifetape to Jim Brigham.

Chapter 11

ELECTRODES.
Om . . .
Syringe.
Om mani . . .
Taping.
Om mani padme . . .
Falling backward into time . . .
Om mani padme um . . .
Falling . . .

Davy moved the coffeepot closer to the coals with his toe. The wind was cold where it found its way through a crack between two logs. *Have to chink that tomorrow.* Davy had had all of the cracks chinked, but some were always falling out. The storm outside was still building, though the winds were already blowing a gale. Rain thundered down on the corrugated-metal roof. He looked again, but there were no leaks; he had pitched the last one a week earlier.

Patrick Singer moaned in his sleep. Davy's eyes sought him out in the dimness. Only the fireplace shed any light on the one-room cabin. Again Davy's father muttered, but it was nothing intelligible.

I should get Michael or Sarah to sit with him tomorrow night, Davy thought. He had hardly slept for three nights now, since Pa had taken the fever. The doctor could do nothing, or said that he could not. You could never be sure with a Gentile.

That thought almost made Davy smile. He had been a professing agnostic for six months now, but his prejudices still made him side with his own people, misguided as he now thought them to be.

No, he would not get Michael's help yet. There was no reason he could not catnap; after all, the doctor said there was nothing he could do. Only a matter of time. And he had no intention of placing himself in Michael's obligation, no matter how hard it became to take care of Pa. Michael already blamed him for Pa's condition, saying that his defection had taken the heart out of the old man.

Seventy years of dredging a bare living out of the unyielding Ozark soil had killed him—was killing him. Not anything Davy had done. He knew that, and someday he might thank Michael for turning what might have become guilt into less harmful anger. Someday, but not now.

The coffeepot had begun to gurgle, so Davy poured himself a cup. Chicory. He had developed a taste for real coffee during his time at school, but there was no affording it now.

He ought to mop Pa's face again, but somehow he couldn't bring himself to disturb him. While he was sleeping, he was in less pain. Davy let the bitter brew slip down his throat.

It was never easy being a youngest son. When his brother Michael had been his age, there had been an older brother (Patrick, Jr., now dead) and Davy to help, and Pa had been younger and stronger. And Ma had been alive to give all their labor some meaning. But Pat was dead, Ma was dead, Pa was dying, and Michael had married and moved away. That was the only bitter consolation left to Davy—that he did not have to put up with Michael's sneering superiority. The work that fell on Davy was too much and the farm was falling into disrepair. He no longer planted the highest hectares, and weeds grew around the home place, but there were only so many hours in the day, and it took them all just to do what he did. And he still had to tend to Pa.

There was a momentary lull in the storm; then the rain struck the roof with redoubled fury, accompanied by the bell-like thrumming of hail. Patrick Singer cried out momentarily, then subsided. "Anne!"

There was no Anne Singer to comfort him now. Davy felt the first stirring of tears. Pa would not last out the night.

And his last six months had been a torment. And it was all Davy's fault.

His chicory was forgotten, grew cold in the cup, as his mind skittered back down the days.

Davy and his father could hear the singing begin as they crossed the meadow. Across the verdant hillside the sun was setting over the Gulf of Texas, and below them the seaport of Little Rock sent up foulness that seldom reached these heights. That was somehow symbolic of the Millennium that men should work on as if nothing untoward had happened, blissfully unaware that the Reign had already begun; yet that the outpourings of their pointless labor could not reach or unsettle the Elect. That thought had given Davy a feeling of superiority before, but of late he had been drawn increasingly toward those same fleshpots.

The church was of stone and logs, built with more care than most of the members' houses. In winter an oildrum stove made it a pleasant refuge against the fog and dampness of the Ozark Island, and often in summer the elders would build an arbor of poles, roofed with chicken wire and rushes. There the services would proceed by the afterglow of the setting sun, occasionally enlivened as bats chased June bugs among the packed church members.

Now it was late fall. The leaves still clung forlornly to the jack oaks, dead but unburied. The oildrum stove had brought the temperature up inside and Davy shed his jacket gratefully.

The Singer cabin and farm were five kilometers west of the meetinghouse. They could neither fertilize nor irrigate, the latter because of inclement geography, the former for reasons of doctrine which had never been clear to Davy. Life had been easier before his brothers left to make lives of their own. Of course, he or his father could have taken a job in Little Rock, but the Elect did not mingle with the Gentiles.

That is, they did not except when compelled by law. Four mornings a week, Davy walked down to the town for compulsory schooling. His was the first generation since the Tribulation to do so. Despite legal battles waged by the Church hierarchy, the resurgent Federal government had stood fast on the subject of compulsory education.

There was some singing, some prayer; then the Reverend Powell stepped up to the podium, slapping down his Bible and darting his eyes from face to face. He opened the book, announcing the seventh chapter of the Revelation, a text which Davy did not need a Bible to remember.

"After this I beheld, and, lo, a great multitude, which no man could number, of all nations, and kindreds, and people, and tongues, stood before the throne, and before the Lamb, clothed with white robes, and palm leaves in their hands."

Only the Gentiles still doubted that the Cataclysm had been Armageddon, or that the years following had been the Great Tribulation. Davy could not appreciate the fear that the Revelation of St. John had struck into Fundamentalist congregations like this one before the Cataclysm. Even the saintly John's description of blood running to the "depths of a bridle bit" could not rival the reality of nuclear war; nor were the "beasts" loosed in the last days anything but pale reflections of the mutations which had plagued the earth these last two centuries.

"*And one of the elders answered, saying unto me, 'What are these which are arrayed in white robes? And whence came they?'*

"*And I said unto him, 'Sir, thou knowest.'*

"*And he said to me, 'These are they which came out of the Great Tribulation, and have washed their robes, and made them white in the blood of the Lamb.' *"

Vaguely, Davy wondered what it would have been like to hear those same verses with Armageddon before him and without the certainty that he was among the white-robed Elect.

"*Therefore are they before the throne of God, and serve him day and night in his temple; and he that sitteth on the throne shall dwell among them.*

"*They shall hunger no more, neither thirst anymore; neither shall the sun light on them, nor any heat.*

"*For the Lamb which is in the midst of the throne shall feed them, and shall lead them unto living fountains of waters; and God shall wipe away all tears from their eyes.*"

Davy had recently come across an ancient book in the archives of the school library which described the pre-Tribulation fundamentalist sects, including transcripts of sermons preached before the last days. They had quoted these same scriptures in their description of the Millennium to come. Only they had taken them literally, and Davy could attest that even in the Millennium a man still hungered the thirsted, and the Lamb fed men as he always had—by providing seed and soil, rain and sun. The rest, as always, was up to man.

Reverend Powell shut his Bible and Davy turned off his ears, though he was careful to look attentive as always. His mind slipped naturally into well-worn paths of perplexity. There were contradictions between the teachings of the church and the teaching he received at the Federal school, contradictions he could not resolve; but what was worse, those contradictions had made him sensitive to other contradictions *within* his religion. The difference between the Revelation's description of the Millennium and the reality he perceived was one such, but there were other, more pressing problems. How, for instance, could a God who was both all powerful and entirely loving have allowed Armageddon to take place?

Davy could not know that he was independently posing the age-old mystery of omnipotence and omnibenevolence co-existing in an imperfect world. Nor would he necessarily have recognized the question thus posed; his education to date had been rudimentary at best. He only knew that there was something seriously wrong with the beliefs of his elders.

Davy had always been close to his father, and could ask his advice on any other question, but not this one. Instinctively, he shied away from verbalizing his uncertainty, knowing that it was one subject with which Pat Singer could not cope. Two decades later, when time and death had utterly sundered them, Dave would recognize this as his father's own defense against disbelief.

"Just the other day a man from Little Rock stopped me on the street." Some change in the rhythm of Reverend Powell's delivery caught Davy's ear. "He said to me, 'Powell—Powell, how can you call this the Millennium when you Millennialists spend your whole lives dragging a bare living out of the soil?' Then he quoted to me these same scriptures.

"Brothers and sisters, no Christian ever quoted scripture half so well as the Devil.

"I said to him, 'Mr. Jones, there are times to be clever, but questioning God's word is *never* clever. I don't know why God chose to speak in physical terms in the scriptures, but I know that I never hunger after righteousness, nor thirst after truth. He dwells with me every day, here in the temple of my heart, and he has cleansed me in living fountains of grace. He feeds me on his word, and, Sir, he has wiped *every* tear from my eye; and I rejoice in his daily presence!'

"What care I if my belly is empty, if my heart is full? And what care I if God's enemies twist his words, taking symbolic statements as literal truth? What care I if they hurl lies in my face, as long as I have truth in my heart?"

A chorus of "Amens" followed as Powell broke off on a high note. He paused artfully, leaning across the podium, letting silence fill up the room; then he went on more softly.

"The Devil is wily and tireless. Even now, chained in the bottomless pit, he still influences the unwary. This poor man, whom I have called Mr. Jones, was not satisfied.

"Brothers and sisters, the Devil is *never* satisfied.

"He said to me, 'Powell, if God is all-loving and all-powerful, why did he allow the Cataclysm and the pestilence of mutations which followed?'

"Brothers and sisters, the Devil is clever. He asks telling questions; be sure, he is no fool.

"I said, 'Mr. Jones, I don't know.'"

His voice had fallen to a whisper, but no ear missed a word.

"'*I* don't know. But God knows, Mr. Jones,' I said. 'I'm only a man. I don't know why God does what he does, but I know that it is to my ultimate good.'

"'And how do I know? Because God loves me. He said in His Book that He loves me, and I believe Him.'

"That's faith, brothers and sisters. Faith.

"It's faith that raises man above the animals and faith that raises Christians above the Gentiles.

"But if I could understand everything, how could I have faith? If I understood, why would I need God?

"I rejoice in my frailty, my ignorance, for only through it do I know the glorious feeling of utter, childlike faith in my Father."

He raised his hands and the congregation rose to sing. Davy rose with them, his heart pounding.

He could not believe! All his life he had accepted, passively, but he could not *believe*, actively. To do so was to deny self, to deny his own value and importance, and he could not. Rather, he *would* not.

In the moment that he refused belief, all the paradoxes and perplexities stood revealed, solved. What had seemed so monolithic from within was shot through with idiocy and honeycombed with rot when viewed from without. The superstructure of doctrine crashed down around him in one warm moment of knowing.

It was all lies.

There was no Millennium; there had been no Armageddon, only madmen in conflict. There was no God. There was only man and his frailty reaching out for eternal life in the face of irrevocable death.

With assurance so utter that it thrilled him even as it stripped him of his defenses, Davy Singer knew—*knew*—that there was only himself and death, black death, waiting at the end of the corridor of his life.

Light slanting through the cabin window woke Davy. He had started out remembering, then had slept, and he was uncertain when the remembering had ceased and the dreaming had begun.

The months after his negative conversion had been rough. He had told his father of his new feelings, trusting him to understand, but in that he had underestimated his father's own needs. There had been no understanding, just bitter recriminations.

Shaking sleep from his mind, he rose and went to check his father's fever. He was dead.

It took several seconds for the enormity of the event to sink in; then Davy pressed his ear hesitantly against the old man's chest. There was no heartbeat, no sound of breath.

Davy backed away from the bed, torn between the need to run for a doctor and his unwillingness to leave his father. But as he watched the open eyes and slack mouth, he realized that it did not matter. He could go or stay, but the dead stay dead.

He went back to the bed and reached out to close his father's eyes. The flesh was warm and he jerked back his hand. Suddenly uncertain, he tapped his cheek lightly. The head rolled sideways on lax muscles and Davy jerked back again, spasmodic shivers taking him. He reached out again; found that he could not touch that dead, warm skin; and drew the blanket over his father's head, instead.

Believing in the Millennium, he had worked his life away, knowing few rewards for all his labor. Believing in an afterlife, he had died secure. But he was just as dead as an atheist would have been.

Just as dead as Davy would someday be.

Somehow, almost subconsciously, Davy had expected some great revelation at this inevitable moment; some sign that his agnosticism was merely the foolishness of youth. He had secretly hoped for such a sign; but there was nothing, just an empty husk and the sound of wind moaning about the eaves.

There were tears then, but there was something more—the beginning of a slow burgeoning terror that would pursue him throughout his life.

Chapter 12

NIRGHAZ'S PLANE ARROWED DOWN-
ward and landed at a minor, deserted military airstrip
near Ranchi. Kantikar's much larger plane, a converted airliner, sat at the end of the runway. There were no
lights anywhere and the nearest building was two
kilometers away at the opposite end of the runway. A
cordon of armed guards surrounded the Premier's
plane.

Kantikar was dictating when Nirghaz wheeled himself into his suite, so he waited quietly until he had
finished. Then Kantikar turned to him with a grave
face. Rarely had he ever greeted Nirghaz without at
least an attempt at a smile.

"What is it, Grandfather?"

"Bhargava! He is pressing me closely. What luck did
you have in Medina?"

"None. They talk and talk, make promises and stall.
But they will not halt construction of their bomb
platform."

Kantikar sighed and passed his hands over his eyes.
He felt very tired and old. "Thank you, Nirghaz. You

might as well go to Deliac now, and get on with your regeneration. I don't think we will be negotiating for a while, but stay handy. If I need you, I will need you instantly."

"What will you do?"

"What can I do! I will launch the Nehru."

Although his orders did not call for it, General Ullah treated them as an emergency. For six minutes the base was a scene of carefully choreographed pandemonium.

The dome drew back, allowing the thin layer of soil and rock that had camouflaged it to fall down into the hangar; no matter, the hangar would not be used again. In a few seconds it would be irradiated beyond recall. Within the bunker, steel and concrete doors were closing.

Ullah was ready to launch; had his orders been more urgent, he would have done so regardless of the danger to those he left behind. As it was, he had merely been ordered to "enter orbit and achieve the destruction of the Medinan bomb platform, after giving adequate opportunity for the evacuation of Medinan personnel", so he waited while the living quarters were properly sealed. He was not impatient. He had waited four long years for this moment and he did not intend to lose a chance to scramble on the real thing. It was good for discipline.

Minutes ticked by as Ullah lounged in his command chair. Only he knew their orders; the others might think anything. Their tension could be felt; good enough! Ullah knew exactly what he had to do and how he intended to go about it. Let the others wonder and wait; that, too, was good for discipline.

The last light turned green and Ullah gave his orders. The Nehru spurned the earth.

She fell skyward at an easy two gravities. The bunker which caught the first seconds of blast was instantly contaminated. As the Nehru arrowed skyward the dome closed again, this time permanently, and the personnel left behind were already evacuating. Having served its purpose, it would now be a radioactive tomb for any who lingered there.

High above India, a Medinan spy satellite caught the flare of the Nehru's torch, photographed it, and caught the radioactive spoor she laid across the upper atmosphere. Relays clicked and men scrambled. Within minutes the air above Medina was full of planes and three military rockets were being rapidly counted down. India was quicker and more certain, for she had the advantage of foreknowledge. In Bombay, Kantikar was quietly spelling out terms to his Medinan counterpart.

General Ullah was all business; for the moment his political hopes were forgotten. For the moment he was an Indian, not a partisan, and he wholeheartedly agreed with his present orders, save for the unnecessary evacuation clause. The Nehru slipped firmly into orbit a mere fifty kilometers behind the incipient Medinan platform. The Nehru's sensors had already told Ullah of the triple launch from Medina, and the massive battle computer had already given him preliminary data from which to form a decision. He spoke softly into the microphone at his elbow and three darts were launched.

The Medinan rescuers were modified high-atmosphere planes mounted atop booster rockets. The Indian darts were of a different breed. With stubbier wings and no landing gear, they were designed to be launched from and serviced in the Nehru. They were entirely in their element, which the Medinan planes were not, and they had the advantage of attacking from above.

The first dart met its counterpart with a blast of unguided 30-millimeter rockets that tore through his LOX and LH tanks, destroying him in a rapidly expanding fireball. The second dart found himself facing a heat-seeking missile, killed his torch, and leaped down the Medinan plane's throat. Forced to an evasive maneuver, the Medinan lost the offensive for a fatal half-second, and in that time the dart flashed past and launched a missile of his own from his single rear-facing missile mount. The Indian pilot waited until the Medinan missile had homed in on the resultant fireball before he dared to relight his torch.

The third dart pilot fired four heat-seeking missiles from long range and killed his torch, allowing the Medinan missiles to slip harmlessly past. He was a few years older than his two companions and that much more cautious. He knew what they had yet to learn—that a commander wants results, not heroics.

The destruction of the Medinans had taken only minutes, and Ullah was well pleased. Three kills, no losses, and no darts had dipped so deeply into the gravity well that they would be unable to rejoin the Nehru. Good!

Ullah turned back to the task at hand, seeking out his radio communications officer with his eyes. He got a nod; contact had been established. "Proceed," he ordered, and the officer began to read a demand for surrender in carefully worded Pashto. For the first time, Ullah had time to look at the Medinan platform. It was at a very early stage of construction. There were a pair of empty cargo rockets which had obviously been converted into living quarters and a spider web of girders, the ultimate shape of which could not be determined.

"General, the commander says that he and his men have no way of abandoning the station. They go down in the rocket that brings up their replacements. They ask that we wait until their people send up a rocket, or take them on ourselves."

Ullah considered. It was likely that the man was telling the truth, and yet . . .

A relief rocket could disguise any number of

unpleasant things, such as a nuclear warhead, and there was no way he was going to let any Medinan aboard the Nehru. He gave orders and a dart was launched.

It accelerated directly toward the station, taking no heed of the necessity for rendezvous. It was a drone. The radio broke into protest, but Ullah couldn't understand Pashto and he waved aside the translation. Abruptly, the communication ceased and a moment later he saw the flare of a rocket at the platform. He smiled.

He had been right; they had had a rescue capsule. Not that it mattered to Ullah; and not that it was going to do them any good. They had waited too long.

The drone was still accelerating when it reached the platform, and the computer, faster and surer than a human pilot, detonated it. For a space of minutes a new sun hung in the heavens, but Ullah saw none of it. The computer had cut the viewscreen, and when it came back to life there was only a faintly glowing, rapidly expanding sphere of vaporized steel.

Ullah scanned his boards. His orbit was stable within bounds of reasonable error and there was no immediate menace from the surface. At his order, the communications officer transmitted a coded signal that meant mission accomplished. Then he let his tense muscles relax and sent his orderly for tea. He would wait now for further orders or a new attack from the surface, neither of which was likely to materialize for several hours.

It never occurred to him that, for the first time in two centuries, man had once again sent a nuclear weapon to destroy his fellowmen.

Chapter 13

RAM LAL SRINIVAS WAS ADVISOR TO AND confidant of Sri Karji. He alone of all Kantikar's advisors called him by his first name, a point upon which Kantikar had made an almost tyrannical insistence. "Ram Lal," he had said, "I *have* to have someone I trust well enough to kick me in the ass when I make a fool of myself."

Srinivas had brought his good shoes to the conference.

Kantikar was pacing the rug, muttering to himself, both sure signs of uncontrollable anger. "Why, Ram Lal? Why? How could that *chamar* misconstrue his orders to include using nuclear weapons against the Medinan platform? It has no precedent in warfare. He used a cannon to kill an ant."

"The Congress won't see it that way, especially after your last speech on the danger the Medinan station posed."

"Dammit, man, the threat was potential, not imminent! No, there's no excuse. I'm relieving him of his command."

Srinivas said nothing.

"Don't tell me you agree with that . . . that . . . " He ground to a sputtering halt, unable to think of an expletive powerful enough to convey his utter disgust. "Jogendranath, think! How are you going to relieve him?"

"Huh? Oh, my God!"

"Precisely. You did a very foolish thing in your haste to launch the Nehru. You should have taken away his command years ago, and now you'll have to pay the price. If you try to relieve him now, Bhargava will make him out as a hero, *quoting your speeches,* and then call for a vote of confidence—which I don't think you could weather. And if you did, and Ullah refused to be relieved . . . then what? Are you going to throw rocks at him?"

For the space of five minutes Kantikar did not move, but he was thinking frantically. Finally, he raised his head and snapped orders through his intercom that would set his plans in motion. Srinivas nodded agreement. "Yes, Jogendranath; for the moment General Ullah has to be a hero. Meanwhile, if you will excuse me, I have to see what we can salvage from this fiasco."

After Srinivas left, Kantikar went to his bedroom. There he stripped, lowered his thin body into the lotus position, and let his consciousness go. He found it unusually hard tonight, and his meditation did not seem to leave him refreshed. He considered sleep, then slipped into a *dhoti* and walked out into his private garden. There he lay back on a chaise and stared at the stars. His privacy was secure; there were guards to make sure that that was so.

He had erred grievously. As in the affair at Mahmet, he had erred. He briefly considered Nirghaz's plight and set it aside. What could be done for Nirghaz, he was doing. Indeed, he was diverting some of his country's resources at a critical time. That was wrong, but the resources diverted were small and he simply chose to ignore this self-admitted error. He did not try to justify it; he accepted, and set it aside.

His real error at Mahmet had been in thinking that an airstrike with conventional weapons would shake Medinan intentions and prevent further, worse bloodshed in the future. It had not. Now he had let one of his political enemies gain control of his country's most powerful weapon. Another error, potentially much worse than the first.

He was getting old. No; he *was* old. His body was frail and wasted and tired; his mind was tired, as well. If he could have done so, he would have quit years ago.

But he could not. Indian politics had always been highly personalized. He was Sri Karji, a national hero. The bloc he headed had no identity except as the followers of Sri Karji—he doubted that it would survive his passing. Only by remaining personally in command could he prevent Bhargava from rising to power. He had beaten back eight attempts on his power in the last decade, and each vote of confidence had left his position weaker than it had been before.

Bhargava represented a militancy that Kantikar could see only as India's damnation, and perhaps the world's. If nuclear weapons were used again . . . Already mankind was teetering on the brink of oblivion from sterility.

There was no drawing back from power and no way to pass on the power he had accrued. Nirghaz should have been his successor, but Nirghaz had the eternal stigma of a Muslim father. He would not survive—politically—Kantikar's passing. Yet even Nirghaz was no longer a proper inheritor of Karji's mantle; he had turned inward in his bitterness. He was no longer one to sacrifice his life for the good of his people—and that, more than the loss of his legs, was the change that crippled him in Kantikar's opinion.

Kantikar's body asserted itself then, and his wandering thoughts wound down into sleep.

Colonel Mohan Bhatt, Commandant of the Deliac Air Force base, waited until a servant had answered the door, then followed him into an inner room. The master of the house did not greet him or even admit his presence. If questioned, he would say that he had not been there.

Gopal Bhargava, leader of the Loyal Opposition, met him in the inner room. The drapes were drawn. Bhargava waved Bhatt to a chair and offered him a drink, then raised his eyebrows. "Well?"

This was the moment Bhatt had dreaded, but there was little he could do to make it easier. "I haven't much to give you. Kantikar has thrown a net of security around that project that a rat couldn't get through. I've tried transferring some of my men in there—no luck— and bribing the men he brought in. Nothing. I've thrown everything I dare against him and it just bounced. If I try any harder, the whole world is going to know it."

Bhargava nodded, unperturbed. "Don't worry about it, Mohan. Kantikar has more trouble in Bombay than he can handle. What do you think of Ullah's actions?"

"Outstanding, and about time. Will the Medinans fight?"

"I don't know. I doubt it—not yet, anyway. Ullah did well—I can't believe that Kantikar left him in command; his opinions were never very well hidden."

"It's just another bit of proof to me that the old man is slipping."

"Perhaps. Anyway, I intend to press him very closely now. Either he will carry on in a manner more suitable to the leader of India, or he will censure Ullah. In the case of the latter, we'll have him out on a vote of no confidence."

"Why not try something more direct?"

"Assassination? Bhatt, you have to learn to say what you mean."

"All right—assassination."

Bhargava swirled the pale liquid in his glass and considered. "Not now, Mohan. Our last attempt was a dismal failure. The only thing that saved us was the overeagerness of the Premier's guards. If that bastard had lived to talk, we'd both be facing a firing squad." He smiled at his nephew. "You don't really want that, do you?"

His name was Ahmed, but those who knew him called him Ram Lal. He had worked on the Ganga Project; he had tried to build a bomb into the speaker's podium where Sri Karji was to speak, but had failed. Then he had watched with satisfaction as one of Bhargava's agents had shot at Kantikar, and had been disgusted that he had done such a poor job of it. Of course, the Indian government had blamed the assassination attempt on Medina, but Ahmed knew better. A Medinan agent would not have missed; Ahmed knew this, for he was a Medinan agent.

Now he waited along the route his contacts assured him Kantikar's motorcade would take the following morning, caressing a Traktonic Mark X. Ten rounds, rocket powered, heat seeking, and explosive. Medinan agents were thorough.

Chapter 14

RAMADAV HAD WARNED HIM OF WHAT to expect. The taping would be no different from any other session, with the exception that he would be running down the memories of the last few months, reliving (without being aware that he dwelled in memory, rather than in reality) his decision to transmigrate; re-arguing with himself, hearing again the inner debate, and finally concluding again that he would do it. In fact, he realized, at this moment he might be in the sensory deprivation tank remembering, rather than sitting in his room thinking these thoughts for the first time. It was a disconcerting consideration.

All that was familiar now. He had gained a great respect for the powers of memory over these last months; though each session overrode the previous one, and he could no longer so clearly recall his childhood or his adolescence, he could remember how he had felt after the taping sessions and he remembered the feeling of remembering. Memory of a memory. Such confusion. He felt depressed and old then, and drew his cloak tighter about him.

What would be different (or was different if this were memory replaying rather than the original actuality) about this taping session was that he would wake up with his new body. Against that, Ramadav had been most stringent in his warnings, for it would not be a pretty sight. His present body was merely truncated; the clone body was a wasted, white wreck. It had never seen the sun; never felt the pull of gravity. He would be bedfast for weeks or months as he gradually, painfully brought it up to health. Furthermore, it would be a younger body, that of a fifteen-year-old—old enough to contain his experiences, having the proper hormonal balance, but still young and resilient enough to take the necessary recovery regimen. Even after he had recovered, he would have the experiences of a man crammed into the body of a boy.

To run again. To lie with a woman again. To be free from the attendance of nurses; to be free of pity. To meet men and women as an equal again. The need burned within him, overpowering his hesitation so that he longed for the coming day and forgot his fear for a moment.

Dave stepped outside just as the nurse was helping Husain transfer to the wheelchair. Nirghaz looked up and grinned. "This will be the last time I have to do this." Dave could see worry and anticipation warring in his expression. He took the handles of the chair and wheeled him inside.

"Have you had any trouble with Bhatt?" Nirghaz asked.

"No, not really. He's tearing his hair out because there is a secret on his base that he doesn't know about."

"Don't be too sure. I saw him this morning when I came aboard and he said, 'How much do you think you'll eventually pay for recovery?' He seems to know pretty much what we are up to."

Dave thought about it for a minute. "I suppose the

type of equipment we've imported tells him something, and my research papers to date are freely available to anyone who is curious. Still, there is nothing he can do as long as your grandfather is Premier."

Husain nodded. "Indian politics is funny. It often works itself out along family lines. Bhatt is a nephew to the opposition leader in Congress."

"Really? That's some coincidence."

"Ramadav! Come up for air; get your head out of that computer and take a look at the real world. There is no coincidence involved when a half-competent light colonel gets boosted in rank and is given a major post to command within a month of his uncle becoming opposition leader."

Dave shrugged again, totally uninterested.

Shashi met them at the door of the lab, with a smile for Nirghaz. There was no smile for Dave. Nirghaz turned aside, asking, "Ramadav, are you sure that I can't look at the body I am about to inhabit? It might make my transition easier."

Dave shook his head. "Sorry."

"Where is Sri Karji?" Shashi asked. Dave had said nothing, but he was also surprised that Kantikar was not on hand for the culmination of Nirghaz's restoration.

"He wanted to be here, but he has to give a speech in Udaipur at the headquarters of the Panch-ab project. It's an essential appearance."

The lab assistants helped Nirghaz out of his clothing. The shame he always felt was more than mere reaction to nakedness, but it was a small thing to endure in recompense for what would be his. Dave carried over the helmet. It was made from a life cast, its pliable interior molded to every line and plane of his head. He shivered each time it was slipped over his face, cutting off all contact with the world beyond. Shashi always gave him a moment to regain his composure before donning it; but today Dave was handling it, and he was all business.

Darkness; a fumbling and tugging as the helmet was tightened. Tiny nipples spread his nostrils and the air had a faint metallic tang. That changed to a subtle perfume as the hoses were hooked up to the airflow monitor. There was a slap on his shoulder—Ramadav, no doubt—and hard hands caught him under the armpits.

Warm fluid; a sensation of drowning. The saline solution was of the same temperature as his skin and it buoyed him up. Within moments the sensation of wetness had passed and he was floating free, insulated from heat, light, and the pull of gravity. He heard a crash; then there was only the roar of water and the susurration of air. Later there was another crash. The outer tank had been filled and sealed, cutting off all sound, save the sound he himself chose to make. The umbilical was long enough to suspend him in the center of the tank, five meters from any wall. He moved his hands, but there was no sensation in them. Only proprioception and cognition remained—and hearing, for the pounding of his own heart had become loud in his ears.

And scent, for some chemical had been introduced into his air stream and consciousness began to fail. Then there was the same sure voice—Shashi's voice— that always banished his claustrophobia and guided him back to the appropriate moment so that he began to remember. . . .

Dave sat before the computer, his hands flashing over controls as complex as the cockpit of a fighter jet. Shashi stood before the monitors of the clone, testing, and bringing it up to the threshold of consciousness so that it could receive the memories that were to be its.

The motorcade wound into view and Ahmed flipped off the safety, bringing the nylon stock up to his cheek. The crosshairs fell on the lead vehicle and held as it slipped past, as a second slipped past and as the bubble-topped tram bearing Kantikar rolled into view. He pressed the firing stud. The projectile said *fisssss,* fading, and the dome of the tram was lost in a burst of flame. Ahmed fired again and again, knowing that one projectile alone would not burst that dome. The ground around him exploded from the guard's return fire. He lost his sight picture, rolled aside, and waited three interminable heartbeats. The smoke began to clear (he had chosen a hill overlooking the ocean for the sake of its breeze) and he fired again. In the brief moment allotted, he had seen that the dome was cracked.

Then the world was torn apart around him and he knew nothing more.

The computer could transfer taped memoies to the clone at the same time that it took new memories from Nirghaz, but Dave waited an hour until there was no chance that the taping would abort. Then he gave the computer the okay and the first tape, taken months earlier, began to print itself onto the soft flesh of the clone's empty mind. It began to experience Nirghaz's childhood.

It would take as many hours to transcribe the tapes as it had required to make them, and though the process was a thousand times faster than the original accumulation of those memories, it would still take better than one hundred fifty hours.

Five hours passed before Dave relaxed. The final taping was through. Nirghaz lay quiescent in the sensory deprivation tank; he would remain there until the memories were transcribed to his clone. Then Dave would cut his oxygen.

This Shashi knew, yet as the moment approached she began to fear. It would not come until the transcription was completed some six days hence. Still . . .

She had pondered long over the implications of the

coming transference and its meaning for Nirghaz's *atman*. Would the essence of what was Nirghaz pass from one body to the next when the first was extinguished? She thought that it would, but who could be certain?

There was a disturbance in the tank that Shashi tended. The clone had begun to writhe as it experienced life vicariously, but it was well restrained. Shashi checked all the dials, then realized that she was holding her breath.

Dave left his console, stretching hugely, and walked around the room, checking monitors. Nirghaz's broken body lay secure in its deathwomb. His memories were quiescent in a sleep beyond sleep while transcriptions of those same memories were being fed to his clone. There was an electric tension in the air. Shashi sought Dave's attention with her eyes, but he was totally absorbed.

The clone jerked, trying to cry out through a mouth that had never known speech, and was restrained by the helmet. Dave leaned over Shashi's shoulder, checking monitors, his face as expressionless as the smooth wall of the tank.

Shashi walked away, leaving him to watch the progress. She should sleep now. Nirghaz had agreed to the project. He was her friend and he had walked (she shivered at that unintended thought) wide-eyed into this; it was her duty to him to carry her end of the process. She should sleep, for one of them had to remain on duty through the coming days, and neither of them would dare leave the room until the transference was completed.

There was a tray of sandwiches on the table. She was not hungry, but she ate, thinking of Nirghaz and of her unborn child.

The assistants had left after helping place Nirghaz in the tank. No eyes but theirs had ever seen this room in action. She let her eyes sweep over the interior of the huge abandoned hangar; pain and loneliness reflected back.

Dave paced like a panther before the monitors, completely unaware of her. His feet scruffed along the floor; the computer hummed; the clone writhed. Otherwise, there was silence.

Chapter 15

SHASHI WAS JERKED AWAKE BY A pounding on the hangar door. Dave looked up in irritation and jerked his head; she went to the door.

"Open up!" It was Bhatt's voice. Shashi turned to Dave instead of answering. He shrugged.

"I can't open up now, Colonel. We are at a crucial point in our experiments. Anyway, you aren't authorized to come here."

"I am now. Open up or I'll have the door knocked down."

Dave cursed and crossed the room. He drew the bolt and faced Bhatt as he shoved in, flanked by armed guards. They scattered around the hangar, searching for other occupants and finding none.

"What the hell do you think you're doing? This is a top-secret project, authorized by the Premier himself."

Bhatt ignored him. "Where is Husain?"

"I ask again, by what authority do you break into a top-secret project?"

Bhatt rounded on him with a look of hatred. "And *I*

ask again, where is Husain? Don't think you can hide behind Kantikar anymore. He was shot this morning by a Medinan agent. He is dying and the government has resigned. Bhargava is in power for the duration of the emergency, or until new elections are held. You are no longer in a protected position, so for your own sake you had better cooperate."

Dave and Shashi exchanged looks of desperation. Why now, of all times?

"Husain is in one of the sensory deprivation tanks," Dave improvised, "undergoing deep hypnotic analysis. This project is designed to bring up everything, however minuscule, he has learned in Medina for computer analysis."

Bhatt looked like a man who had walked full face into a wall. Clearly, he had had some idea of what was going on here, but Dave's instant story was too plausible to ignore. If it were true, he had better tread lightly. His sources had given him a different story, but they could have been wrong.

Dave saw his advantage and took it. "I don't know whose orders you are following, but if you don't keep your troops in control and let Dr. Mathur and me get back to our work, Husain will die, and then you will be in more trouble than you can handle."

Dave turned his back on Bhatt and walked to the computer console. He killed the transcription to the clone. Dave's face was as bleak as Shashi had ever seen it. "What now?" she whispered.

"Nothing. We cancel everything; we tell nothing; but most of all we have to get Nirghaz out of that tank!" He twisted the dial increasing the oxygen flow to Nirghaz's broken body, and cut in the program of music and recorded voices that would lure him back from the sleep that lies on the edge of death.

Music came softly into his ears, followed by voices that seemed to make sense but did not, quite. By the time he had recognized that he was hearing an ordinary conversation with the key words omitted, he was well on his way back to consciousness.

There was sound, a crashing followed by the rush of waters. None of this made a great deal of sense. What Husain could not know was that Dave had introduced a sedative into his bloodstream before awakening him.

. There was a shifting perception of motion and harsh hands dragging him up. There was a hard pressure under his spine and then light, blinding light. Dave swam oddly above him; then there was a pinprick in his arm. Somehow Nirghaz knew that all of this was not as it had been planned, but then darkness took him.

He was still dissociated and confused when he woke up. Slowly he unwound his memories up to the taping and smiled. He had done it! That his subsequent memories were not as he had been coached was of no consequence.

To live again as a man, a whole man!

He opened his eyes. The ceiling was white and he could see little else. He could not feel his new legs, which displeased him. Ramadav had said that he would be too weak to sit up, but he felt like trying. He heaved and nothing happened.

It was as if he were still legless.

He jerked his head up. It was a momentary glance, but he could see the dip in the sheet where his legs should have been.

"*No!*" His soul-deep cry of betrayal rang through the building.

Dave rushed into the room with a soldier at his back. Nirghaz's eyes pleaded with him to say that it was not true, but he could only shake his head. He took Nirghaz's hand, but Nirghaz turned his face away. Bhatt came in running and eyed Dave, commanding, "Do what is necessary, but say nothing!"

Dave ignored him. "Nirghaz, I'm sorry. Bhatt terminated our experiment. Your grandfather was shot this morning and is dying. The government has re-signed."

"If you say one more word, I'll have you thrown out." Dave responded with an obscenity, in English, but it was one that had found its way into many languages and Bhatt recognized it. He gestured and a soldier prodded Dave with his weapon. Dave shrugged and turned away, but Nirghaz saw the tears edging his eyes.

Not betrayed, then, for Ramadav shares my pain. But to fall from such hopes! It is more than I can bear.

Nirghaz looked up at the man who had brought him back to this hated body and cursed him with a fluency and fervor that made all previous criticisms seem like commendations. And Bhatt stood silent through it. There was no certainty that Husain might not be in power again soon, for his importance to the Medinan negotiations was well known.

Kantikar had been hit outside Udaipur and lay now in an intensive care ward there. There was an air force base nearby where Husain landed two hours later in the back seat of a fast fighter. He was met there by a military attaché who filled him in on the details. He tried to listen, if only to take his mind off his crushed hopes. A Medinan assassin had fired on Kantikar's vehicle with an explosive shell rifle, bursting the dome. When the shelling stopped with the assassin's death, they found Kantikar cut and bruised, his heart no longer beating.

The medical officer who always accompanied Kantikar had begun cardiopulmonary resuscitation immediately and he had been rushed to the hospital, but no effort could bring his ancient heart to function without life-support equipment.

They had bypassed his heart and lungs; two thumb-thick tubes protruded from his chest, carrying blood to and from the support system. They caught Nirghaz's eye when he entered the room; blue blood out, red blood back in. A sheet had been pinned beneath Kantikar's chin to shield this from his eyes.

The bed had been raised to make it easy for the doctors to work, and Nirghaz could see little from his wheelchair. He gave curt instructions to a pair of orderlies. They hesitated until the presiding physician snapped, "Do it!" Moments later he was perched on a mobile table with the orderlies supporting him.

Kantikar had been old, but the fire of life had burned bright within him. His devotion to India had been total and duty had kept him strong. This one blow had opened the door to his age and frailty.

His eyes were closed; his skin was like old, brown parchment.

"He called for you a long time. We couldn't give him a sedative or even a pain suppressant. Either one would have weakened his fight for life. He has said nothing now for nearly an hour."

Nirghaz looked down at him and was ashamed that his own great disappointment made it impossible to feel fully the grief of the moment. Jogendranath Kantikar had lived fully, and his death now would be fulfillment, rather than tragedy.

One of the orderlies shifted his weight, obviously bored with holding Husain upright. Suddenly, he burned at his helplessness. All the defenses he had raised against shame and grief were shattered by his brush with reconstruction, and he lay open to the same despair he had faced immediately after the amputation. But worse; then he had not known all the small and great indignities in store for him, and now he did.

Kantikar's eyes opened briefly, then closed again. "Nirghaz?" he whispered so softly that Husain could hardly hear.

"Here, Grandfather."

For a long time he lay quiescent. Then he said, "Today was your day. I should have been with you." Just a hint of a smile. "I would have been better off if I had been."

"You'll be all right. The doctor told me so."

Nirghaz was not sure that he had heard the lie, for he

lay silent for several seconds, then said, "How are your legs? Can you walk again yet?"

Tears streaked Nirghaz's face, for himself and for the old man who thought only of him, even as he lay dying. When he did not reply, Kantikar rolled his head and opened his eyes. Nirghaz felt shame anew as those old eyes saw him supported between orderlies.

"What happened?" For a moment there was fire in his voice, though it was yet a whisper.

There was no way to soften the truth. "The government resigned, and Bhatt terminated the reconstruction."

Anger suffused Kantikar's features. "By Yama, I will not die until I have paid my debt to you and my new debt to Bhatt! Doctor!" But even as he spoke, convulsions shook him and the orderlies caught Nirghaz by the arms and rushed him from the room. As he went, he could hear the cries of nurses and the scampering feet as the emergency team rushed to Kantikar's bedside.

Chapter 16

THE GULLS WHEELED OVERHEAD, EX-
ulting in their freedom and in the brisk sea wind.
Nirghaz watched them cut patterns against the blue
sky. Great clouds were gathering westward out at sea.
Soon it would be the season of the monsoon.

Kantikar was dead.

Nirghaz slipped the lock on his wheelchair and
wheeled it forward to the edge of the cliff. He had sent
his nurse away; he would never have been permitted to
take such a chance otherwise. Far below him the beach
was deserted. That was good, for his purpose.

There were two packages wedged beneath his
seat. He took out the top one, a recorder, and turned
it on.

Bhatt was still holding Ramadav and Shashi, though
he had not dared to retain Husain. Nirghaz had made
arrangements for their release.

A gull landed near him and he spoke harshly to
frighten it away.

"I am making this record," he said into the microphone, "for the sake of my friends and for my own sake, should circumstances make it possible for Ramadav and Shashi to complete the work we set out to do together.

"That which I am about to do is in part an affirmation of faith in you, my friends. In the months we have been together, I have come to have a great affection for you both. You have been good friends in trying times and I wish you the best in the coming confusion. I have made arrangements with some of those in power to make certain of your safety since I will be in no position to do so myself."

He turned off the machine and stared out to sea again. The salt smell was sharp in his nose and the sun felt good. All life was good. For a moment he hesitated, but his hopes had been raised too high to return to the old accommodations.

He dictated a brief summary of events from the moment he woke up from the aborted transmigration, then paused again.

"I know that, if it is humanly possible to do so, Ramadav and Shashi will continue the project and rescue me from my own folly. But if they cannot, my decision remains unchanged. There are some horrors too great to face, and some disappointments too deep to endure."

This time he paused a very long time, staring at the gulls that circled overhead. Then he said softly, "Shashi, I love you. And you, Ramadav. Be happier in one another's company than you have been of late."

He stared down at the beach with a cold emptiness inside him, than made a final entry. "Life, I love you. Too much to see you broken."

He motioned for his nurse, then sent him to carry the recorder back to the tram at the base of the hill. When he was well along the way, Nirghaz took out the second package and unwrapped it. He had made it himself and knew its capabilities. There was a simple switch built into one end of the casing.

He looked up again at the gulls soaring free and flipped the switch.

The explosion tore him apart and hurled his body to the beach below.

Chapter 17

DAVE PACED THE FLOOR, OCCASIONALLY slamming his fist into the wall. It had been their bedroom; now it was their prison. Shashi sat with her face turned toward the wall, her hands folded protectively across her belly. Three days had passed without word of the world beyond that cubicle. Three times daily they were fed; otherwise, they were ignored.

It was afternoon when they came for Dave, giving no explanation for their coming. Two soldiers entered, ordered him out, and slammed the door in Shashi's face, leaving her alone with her fear.

Bhatt waited for him in his office. The impassivity with which he had masked himself was no longer present. Without preamble or pretense, he said, "Kantikar is dead. Now that you have no one to speak for you, don't you think it's about time that you explained about the experiments you have been doing?"

"I already told you more than you are authorized to know."

"You lied," Bhatt said, not angry, but no longer patient. "There is little enough to be learned from your lab notes, but enough to tell that your project was for the transference of the memories of Husain into a new body."

Bhatt had seemed so much the bumbling fool. Dave mentally castigated himself for blindness. Fat, yes, and slow of speech and action, but the mind that hid behind those mild brown eyes was sharp and ruthless.

"What your notes don't tell," Bhatt went on, "are the codes which are the key to the programs in the computer. Short of washing out whole banks of memory, we cannot make it serviceable again for its original purposes. You will give me the codes."

"No."

The skin beside Bhatt's eyes tightened ever so little. "Sri Singh, your project is ended. The government has need of the computer you have been misappropriating. The codes, if you please."

"Bhatt, you had me fooled for a while, but I no longer consider you an idiot." Bhatt never turned a hair. Before he would have flown into a tantrum at that remark, so there was no longer any doubt that the masquerade was over. "You have no intention of erasing the programs in that computer. You want to protect them for the sake of yourself and your superiors."

"All right, so we do. What objections do you have to that? It is your project. Don't you want to see it carried to completion?"

Suddenly wary, Dave said nothing.

"What of Husain? Don't you want to give him back his legs and genitalia?"

"Of course. But I don't trust you—not one little bit. I will insist on safeguards, starting with Shashi's and my immediate release from confinement, if we are to deal with one another."

Bhatt did not argue; instead, he drew a newstat from his desk drawer and tossed it to Dave. Puzzled, Dave opened it and read the headlines that gave the story of Kantikar's death. "Bottom left," Bhatt said, and then

Dave saw the headline that said: HUSAIN COMMITS SUICIDE. Dave read the article through and dropped the stat on Bhatt's desk.

"How do I know that isn't a forgery?"

Bhatt removed a recorder from the same drawer and switched it on. Nirghaz's voice came out, backed by the mewling of gulls. When it had played through, Dave found that moisture had started to form in his eyes and he fought back the display of emotion.

"You heard. He said that he had made arrangements for our safety."

Bhatt nodded. "Srinivas has been on my tail for two days, trying to get me to release you. However, there have been these rumors circulating, rumors that you got the layout of Kantikar's motorcade route from Husain under the guise of taping him and passed it on to the assassin who finally got Kantikar." Despite himself, Dave showed dismay and Bhatt chuckled. "Of course, it may prove that these rumors have no foundation. It all depends on how well you cooperate."

Dave sighed. "What do you want?"

"That's better. Do you want to reconstruct Husain?"

"Of course."

"Can you do it?"

Dave hesitated, but there was no way out. "Yes."

"Good. You will go ahead as planned and we will monitor your actions, but first you will give us the information which your notes lacked."

When Dave returned safe, Shashi's first reaction was relief, but that passed as quickly as it had come when she saw the expression on his face. "What is it?"

"It's Nirghaz. He committed suicide."

"No!"

Dave collapsed into a chair and Shashi knelt beside him. "Karji died, and after that he couldn't face the prospect of going on crippled. He left a recording, stating his reasons and saying that he was counting on us to reconstruct him."

Shashi jerked as if struck. "There's no way we can do that now."

"Yes, there is. I made an agreement with Bhatt to show him how the process works, in exchange for a chance to resurrect Nirghaz."

"You didn't!"

"Why not? I had no reason to keep the process secret."

"But Nirghaz is dead."

"We have his tapes, Shashi, and his clone. Nothing has changed."

"Oh, but it has. His *atman* is gone now."

"Oh, hell!"

"If you resurrect him now, you'll only have a zombie. A walking corpse."

Dave bounced up and began to pace the room, muttering curses under his breath. Shashi stiffened and drew back. He rounded on her, anger flushing his face. "Dammit, Shashi, it isn't for you to say! If you prefer, it isn't for me to say, either; but *Nirghaz* has the last word. He gave the order for his resurrection and I intend to perform it, with or without your help."

"Well, you won't have it."

Their eyes locked for a space of seconds before she turned away from him. "Shashi!" The word was laid against her back like a lash. "Your commitment to principle may be admirable, but what about your commitment to your friends? Nirghaz went to his death depending on us. Do you know what he said in that recording? I can just about quote it, since I thought they might be the last words I would ever hear him say. He said, 'What I am about to do is an affirmation of faith in my friends. I know that if it is humanly possible, Ramadav and Shashi will rescue me from my own folly.'" Shashi winced at the words. "What kind of principles are there that let you betray a trust like that?"

Shashi's shoulders sagged and she turned back to Dave with eyes that showed no more trace of love.

"Tomorrow," she said, "I will help you make your zombie, and then I'm going to walk away from this whole sordid mess and try to forget I ever met you."

After the recorder had snapped off, Bhatt said, "Did you get all that?"

"Yes," Bhargava's reply came over the phone. "I think we can be sure that the woman won't spread what she knows. She hates the whole idea of the resurrection project. If it is successful—and frankly, I have my doubts—this Singh will be a security risk. Can I count on you to take steps?"

"It will be my pleasure, believe me. But why take chances with her and Husain?"

"A good point. Husain will be needed as an example of what the process can do—if it works." Bhargava chuckled then. "Actually the whole thing will probably prove impossible.

"We can keep an eye on the Mathur woman. If she poses a risk later, we will take steps then. But I want Singh out of the way as soon as he finishes with Husain."

Chapter 18

DAVE PUT THE COMPUTER THROUGH ITS checks while Shashi examined the clone. Armed guards stood at the door and an air force scientist sat at his elbow. Shashi came back to see him, her eyes unnaturally wide. Even her feelings toward Dave were set aside for the moment and he felt a touch of fear. "Is there something wrong with the clone?"

She shook her head and he could see that her hands were trembling. "It has partial memory—we were up to age three when Bhatt interrupted us." She swallowed and went on: "It's alive in there, crying in the night and trying to get out."

Dave shivered at the thought.

Memories flowing in the dark—childhood fleeing before adolescence. The clone aged rapidly, each moment adding days to its store of experience. A clumsy young man alone in the dark with an equally clumsy but eager girl. A state banquet; Sri Karji acknowledging him to the world. His mother's harried face when the world

115

*refused to forget that she had married a hated Muslim
and had borne a half-caste child. The girls who would
and the ones who wouldn't. Especially Renana.*

*Working secretly for Karji; the interminable negotia-
tions with men who valued war over peace. The feel of a
horse between his legs as he flashed across a polo field.
The wamth of sunshine and the coolness of the ocean.*

*Then Mahmet, the polo field, the secret negotiations
and the planes tearing the sky. Pain! Amputation!
Despair.*

Hours passed as the memories accumulated. Dave
sent for a sleeping pad and he and Shashi slept in
rotation, one of them always monitoring the clone. A
hospital bed was secured in anticipation of the project's
completion.

*He remembered Dave's briskness as he settled the
helmet in place. He felt again the sensation of drowning
and the gentle onset of sleep as the taping began.*

Pain! Like he had never known before. A body so
new that it had not yet learned to suppress excess
stimuli, and one that had never known the killing pull
of gravity. He almost passed out with the intensity of it
all.

The bed beneath Nirghaz was a torture rack. He
could feel his new limbs, but it was not good. Every
muscle and joint cried out against the unaccustomed
strain of merely living. Finally, he felt the warm,
death-like spread of narcotic from the burning in his
left forearm.

Six times Nirghaz awakened to such pain that he
could not tolerate it, and six times Dave or Shashi sent
him back into the haven of sleep. Each time he was
stronger, for even lying still his body was stressed by
gravity and responded by building new defenses,
blocking the pain and growing tissue. The seventh time
he awakened, Shashi was at his bedside and she sat thus

for an hour, holding his hand, while he lay awake but too spent to talk. Finally, a natural sleep claimed him.

"Your passes, please."

Srinivas handed the M.P. his identification and Bannerjee leaned across him to do the same. The corporal glanced briefly at them, handed them back, and passed them into the base.

As soon as the monopod had passed from sight, he ran to a phone and carried out his standing orders. Bhatt took the call, and left hurriedly, telling his orderly to stall.

So Srinivas had cornered a member of Congress, after all. That would speed things up.

Shashi was sleeping and Dave was sitting at Nirghaz's bedside when Bhatt entered the hangar with a contingent of armed M.P.'s. Bhatt motioned and two soldiers flanked Dave, one taking each arm. "Take him outside."

Dave jerked back uselessly. "Bhatt, quit making an ass of yourself."

"You can't do this!" Shashi shouted. "He hasn't done anything!"

"Restrain the woman. I want a guard set over her and over this one." He motioned to Nirghaz where he lay in the bed.

"Bhatt, you just lost yourself a career," Nirghaz promised. Bhatt did not seem concerned. He turned and followed his men out.

Dave blinked at the brightness of the day outside. The soldiers hustling him along were anything but gentle and he struggled angrily against them. Bhatt smiled. "Let him go." They did so.

"You two come here." The soldiers backed away from Dave, clearly puzzled.

Bhatt stopped smiling. "Men, the prisoner is trying to escape. Stop him."

Dave stood for one heartbeat, shocked into immobility. The soldiers who had held him swung their rifles up. One of them was grinning.

"Bhatt, no! No!"

Flash, sound and impact, simultaneous. He felt the slugs rip into his body.

Shashi screamed and fell forward, clutching her swollen belly. Miscarriage! It was the only thing she could think of, yet what she felt was not pain. It was . . . even as she experienced the feeling, she knew that it was too alien to define. Something had *entered* her; not physically, not with the transience of a lover. Something had permanently grafted itself into her, like the child that lay within her womb.

She felt movement as the fetus was quickened, and suddenly she knew that the shots she had heard heralded the death of Ram Singh, for it was his *atman* that had entered the child within her.

The sky was very blue. There were no clouds. But there was pain, pain, Pain, PAIN!

PART II

India—2223 A.D.

Chapter 19

DAVE WAS DROWNING IN WARM, WET darkness; then there was noise and a rushing of waters, and light, and pain.

The bed beneath his back was a torture rack and his disorientation was complete. He was not in the hangar lab: Where was he? He tried to sit up—could not—and tried to understand it all.

Then he knew, or thought he knew, and he raised his arm. Thin; flaccid white. He let the arm fall.

All the nightmare questions came back to him then, followed by swift oblivion.

Coming up from pain-induced sleep, Dave saw an older woman he did not recognize. She moved with the ease of long experience, adjusting the monitors at the med console, but she did not wear the traditional nurse's white. Her hair was sandy brown, and if there was gray in it, she hid it well. She shimmered and faded.

When next he awoke, he could feel every wrinkle in the sheet and every seam in the mattress beneath, and each tiny irregularity gouged and tore into his body.

It was dark outside the window when he regained consciousness, and he lay quiescent, moaning irregularly as he watched the dark fade toward eventual morning. He willed himself to remain awake until full light, but agony from his twisted spine clawed him down into darkness again.

The woman was back when he awoke the fifth time. She smiled and sat beside him, taking his hand in hers. He tried to speak, but only managed a croak. "Go ahead and try to talk," she said. "You'll get the hang of it quickly enough."

He stared stupidly through her, trying to make sense of the strangeness in her voice; then he realized that she had spoken in English, and he was so accustomed to NaiHind that he had almost forgotten how.

"Who are you?"

She strained to make out the question, then said, "You don't know me, but I am a friend. My name is Angelena Piaget. Anson Piaget is my husband."

The name Piaget was familiar, but it took Dave's foggy brain several seconds to make connections. Anson Piaget was a well-known biologist. Dave had read many of his articles and had once corresponded briefly with him over some technical problem in his research, but had never met him.

"How did you get here?"

"A friend called us in." She seemed amused by the question, but Dave couldn't understand why. He craned his neck, though even that small exertion was answered by pain, and looked around him. He was in a bedroom, not a hospital, and it was obviously a part of some opulent household. The walls were paneled in teak and the windows were wide silled and low, fronting on a garden. He could catch the scent of flowers and could see a hint of color, but his angle was wrong for seeing much more.

He obviously wasn't at Deliac, unless he was in one of the general's bungalows. "Where are we?"

"Orissa."

"What! Why? What happened?"

She patted him gently and said, "That's a long story and you don't have the strength to hear it now." Then she rose to go, saying, "You really don't need someone watching over you every minute, and if I stay you'll exhaust yourself with questions."

"Wait!" he cried at her retreating back. "What is the date?"

"Thursday, the eighth," her voice floated back from the hall.

"Of what year?" he whispered. But if she heard, she didn't reply.

Within an hour, Dave had worried himself back into oblivion, and when he next awoke he was alone. It was obvious that this was intentional. Whatever had happened between his last waking memory and now had apparently been traumatic enough that they wanted him to prepare himself before they broke the news.

He reviewed what he knew and what he could surmise with reasonable certainty. His body was a mess. His arms, when he raised them, were thin and white, and flaccid from disuse. Throwing back the sheet for the first time, he surveyed the wreckage. There was no question; time and disease had not wrought this. He was wearing a body like the one he had grown for Nirghaz, fresh from the S.D. tank and as yet unstressed by living.

Therefore, he had died.

It was not the shock that it should have been. Despite his altered body and an inevitable time displacement, that bone-deep solipsist *I* remained unchanged and he felt no loss of identity.

What year was it?

When he had made his last taping, he had not yet begun to grow a clone of himself, so some time had passed. How much? Six months? A year? Two years? Or longer. Was that what they were conspiring to keep from him?

And who were *they?* Was this "Angelena Piaget" who she claimed to be?

How had he died? The strangeness of the thought made his pain-drugged mind reel. The room was spinning now and his breath was coming in shallow gasps as blackness came in from the edges of his eyes to blot out his thoughts.

When Dave awoke again, James Brigham was sitting at his side.

He had first met Brigham at Roanoke, had chosen him as a mentor while gaining his first doctorate, and had established a close friendship. When Dave had last seen James Brigham, he had been in his early fifties, thin, stoop shouldered, and tending toward a paunch. He was a man who abhorred athletics and his body showed the results.

The mild brown eyes were the same and there was no mistaking that craggy hooked nose. Dave would have known him anywhere, but Jim Brigham had changed immensely. He had lost weight. His paunch was gone and his musculature, though still lean, had firmed to a wiry hardness. His physical attitude was different; even sitting quietly beside Dave's bed, his tiny motions of hand and shifting of body weight were authoritative, even graceful. He no longer radiated the shy withdrawal that had been his trademark.

But all that was secondary. He looked to be about seventy years old.

Dave grimaced and whispered, "Hello, Jim. What year is it?"

"2223."

Dave closed his eyes but he couldn't suppress the shiver that ran through him. Jim leaned close and gripped his shoulders, then simply waited, letting his physical contact bridge the gap between them.

After a while, Dave opened his eyes again and asked in an oddly dispassionate voice, "Where are we?"

"Orissa, in a hill station that once belonged to the Maharaja of Raipur. It is the headquarters now of a small band of people I recruited after your work was published."

"So it was published. I had wondered about that. How did you ever get any periodical to accept something so *outré?*"

"That's a long story."

Dave looked about him, trying to choose among the thousand questions bubbling in him. "Shashi—is she all right? And did Nirghaz get his legs back?"

"Yes and yes. But that's a long story, too." As briefly as possible, Jim Brigham told of the aborted taping, Sri Karji's death, Nirghaz's suicide and resurrection, and Dave's execution.

When he had finished, Dave turned his face toward the wall, trying to assimilate it all. "It seems like a fantasy."

"I know."

"God!" Then he was silent for a long while before asking, "How did you get an organization together to resurrect me, and why did it take twenty years?"

"I think we should save that story until you've sorted out the one I just told you."

"I suppose." His voice was dispassionate, but tears streaked his cheeks and he felt lost and alone. But not so alone as he would feel later when this fantasy became real for him. Jim sat silently beside him for an hour until he drifted into an uneasy sleep.

Chapter 20

THE NEXT MORNING ANGELENA TOOK off after breakfast to leave Dave and Jim alone, and Jim filled in more of the missing years. Twenty years earlier, Dave's letters and lifetapes stopped coming in the mail. Jim found the reason in a small article on an inner page of the *Poona Herald*. Since his copy always came a week late, Dave had already been dead ten days. *What a hell of a way to find out!*

He dropped the stat into his lap, seeing nothing of the room about him. Well, Dave had foreseen it. He had sent letters, notes, and lifetapes. Now he would expect resurrection and Jim was not at all sure that he understood, agreed with, or even believed in the process. New body, old memories, but would it still be the same *person?* Jim did not believe in a soul, exactly, but he was uneasy. It seemed too easy to a man conditioned from birth to accept death as inevitable. But that had been one of Dave's arguments—that men accept death because they are so taught, not out of actual necessity.

Dave's death brought back other memories. Marie had died only four years back, Jim's wife of how many years? Seventeen. She had loved him and made him happy all that time, and together they had borne the common curse of barrenness. Now there was not even a child to remember her by, and when Jim died even her memory would be gone. For the first time in many months, he found himself overcome with emotion. That, too, was unhealthy. When a man stopped feeling, he stopped living.

True to his nature, he had filed Dave's letters in chronological order, and true to his nature, he re-read them all, seeing the gradual transition from hope, to excitement, and then to wariness as the project neared completion. Yet he had never achieved his goal, for Jim had read several weeks earlier of Kantikar's assassination and Husain's suicide.

Or had he succeeded? Husain's suicide would not be a hindrance; indeed, it would remove several sticky moral problems. What had happened between Husain's death and Dave's? Brigham decided to find out.

Next he took out Dave's notes and reviewed them. He had collated them, written an introduction, and prepared them for publication. He had a list of key scientists and government figures who were to receive copies, nearly four thousand in all. Dave had looked forward to having his work censored, and intended to get full dissemination before that happened. It would cost a lot, but Dave had provided for that, too. Soon they would be auditing Dave's institute and would find a goodly sum of rupees missing. As his notes would be missing, or so Jim guessed.

Jim closed his books and leaned back to think. Evening had come as he worked. There was nothing left to do here. Dave's lifetapes were safe, his purloined money was safe, and arrangements had been made with a printer in Calgary to do the work on his book. He had only to turn over the manuscript to set the wheels in motion.

Dave was dead. The realization hit him anew, with a two-pronged attack: One prong was the responsibility he felt for his friend's new life, if, indeed, Dave had not been deluded; the other prong was the sudden realization that Dave was dead *by another's intent*.

If it could happen to Dave, it could happen to James Brigham.

Once Jim would have hesitated, or even dismissed the whole idea as melodramatic. But Dave's increasing worry and ultimate death had brought home to him the knowledge that not all the world worked on calm, peaceful, logical principles.

Excessive caution might prove embarrassing in retrospect, but death would be even more embarrassing. Realizing this, Jim wasted no more time. He slipped the manuscript into a briefcase, followed by Dave's letters. After a moment's hesitation, he added a small revolver and a box of cartridges.

He started for the door, stopped, opened the briefcase, and took out the gun. When he left the house, it lay cold and comforting inside his waistband.

Jim Brigham had rented a house in Calgary, in a lower-class residential district, and it was there he went by a roundabout route.

He left Roanoke on a yawl, under a false name, changed for a schooner in Little Rock under a second false name, and flew from El Paso to Calgary under a third. NorAm had not yet returned to the stage of civilization that required personal identification cards, so he had no trouble leaving any theoretical pursuit behind.

He titled the manuscript *Inquiry into Artificially Induced Immortality* and gave it to a printer. A month later he had four thousand cheaply bound copies on his doorstep. Working alone, it took nearly a week to wrap and address them all, load them into his pickup truck, and set out across NorAm, mailing twenty-five here, fifty there, until they were all gone.

As the copies began to reach their destinations, most of them went unread to a place on a bookshelf, or a box in storage. An unsolicited book on the feasibility of immortality, privately printed, was bound to be received with an overwhelming yawn.

Not all of the books reached their destinations. Some went to incorrect addresses; three of the recipients had died since Brigham compiled the list. These were shuffled around the various postal services and lost.

A few were read, or at least started, by men who recognized the name Ram David Singh. Dave's reputation had been high within certain narrow fields of specialization. Most of these laid the work aside after a few pages, dismissing the contents as mere fantasy.

Of those who read, a few kept open minds and an even smaller number nodded sagely, seeing the feasibility of what they read.

The initial impact of the work was nil, but . . .

In the Andean Republic, in Medina, in India, and in a dozen other countries, the various governments had set watchdogs on the mail coming to those men of science who were considered both valuable and dissident—just the kind of person likely to get onto Brigham's list. Some of the copies were intercepted; of these, many were passed on after being copied, but a few made their way directly to those in charge.

A copy addressed to Juan Hildera was intercepted by the government of the Andean Republic, made its way through several levels of the security hierarchy, bounced over to the religious hierarchy, shocked a priest, astounded a bishop, disgusted a cardinal, and eventually made Pope Juan VIII very angry. He issued a communiqué denouncing *Inquiry* as a work of the devil and threatening excommunication for anyone reading it or advocating its teachings. Poor Juan Hildera had several nights of painful questioning ahead of him before he could convince the Church that he knew nothing of the document. It would probably have gone worse for him if four other top scientists had not turned in copies of *Inquiry* that had been sent, anonymously and unsolicited, to them.

Still, *Inquiry* did not spread rapidly. The Pope's denunciation was carried as a minor story on an inside page—where it was carried at all. The world was too much concerned with imminent nuclear war between India and Medina, and hung on every rumor arising from the negotiations now going on in Kabul.

Yet the rumors had begun. *Inquiry* made the newly revived *Index Librorum Prohibitorum*, and a few people noticed that, rememberd the cheaply bound book stowed—where was it now?—and curiosity got the best of them. Then word began to pass.

Jenner Shildao called up his old friend and constant competitor, Thomas Hillary, to say that he had read *Inquiry* and found it without foundation or merit. Hillary, remembering that he had vaguely heard some controversy about the book, but had not had the time to read the copy someone had sent him, made vague sounds which didn't fool Shildao a bit and later dug out *Inquiry* to see if he could find any virtue in it whereby he could refute his friend. He found much virtue in it, but when he called back a week later, Shildao had mysteriously disappeared.

It had begun.

At first Jim Brigham had felt a little melodramatic. Later he felt like a complete fool, and a contrite one at that, because it was unlikely that he would ever get back his post at Roanoke, or at any other university. He was living now in a cabin high in the Rockies. Before Dave's death, he had stocked the cabin with enough supplies to stand a prolonged siege, so he hiked, fished, lazed in the sun, and worked on a treatise concerning the effects of radiation on *Sturnella neglecta*. Twice a week he drove his aged pickup down from the mountain for magazines.

He stopped feeling melodramatic when every issue of *Science* showed that several more of the men on his mailing list had either died or disappeared. He also stopped fishing and hiking, and started wearing his revolver again.

It had been a hard year and James Brigham had changed much. He no longer carried a paunch; his step was springy now and his eyes wary. He no longer had the look of a scholar, for the world in which he moved was more suited to violence than introspection. His body was wiry now, and his look, feral.

James Brigham had adapted. He was at home with intrigue now and with the eternal imminence of capture, torture, and death. He recruited with care but many of those he would have chosen as companions were either dead or captured. Over three hundred key scientists had disappeared into the unseen but omnipresent vacuum of secret resurrection projects.

Jim met Anson and Angelena Piaget in Malaysia. It was mostly chance that brought them together, for both parties had long been underground. He found Nels Immerson at a château in New Zealand, Dalmar Brown hiding in the slums of Addis Ababa, and Julia Villanova in Bogotá. Nels knew that Nirghaz and Shashi still lived, though daily pursued by the Indian Secret Police.

Five years later Bhargava was ousted from his position as Prime Minister and within a month had disappeared while yachting in the Gulf of Cambay. Bhatt dropped out of sight at the same time. Bhargava's ouster had been over the misappropriation of millions of rupees, and Brigham was fairly certain that those rupees had been used to set up a private resurrection project.

By that time, it was as if the earth had swallowed up *Inquiry* and any of those who might have profited by the knowledge it offered. There was no way of knowing how many secret resurrection projects there were, or how many others were underground like Jim and his companions, but the need for secrecy made it hard for them to get the supplies they needed to set up their own labs. Once they began in a run of pre-Cataclysm bunkers in the Atlas Mountains, but two of the newest recruits to the project disappeared and one of them turned up in an alley in Casablanca with his throat cut. Jim and his friends followed the better part of valor and abandoned the equipment they had accumulated just before they were raided.

A year later, Gopal Choudry was found floating in the Bay of Bengal. Nirghaz supplied that information in one of his infrequent meetings with Brigham.

Nels Immerson split with the group and set himself up as an importer in Raipur. Six years and one near-fatal heart attack later, he came back to the fold, convinced that Dave's techniques were his only key to survival. By that time his import business was flourishing, and he had bought the hill station. Jim and his refugees set up there, using Nels's money and using his business as a front through which to order supplies.

Nirghaz supplied the cell culture for Dave's resurrection. It was taken from Chandra Ayyar, Dave's clone-son by Shashi, now a grown man.

Chapter 21

DAVE HAD BEEN "ALIVE" FOR JUST OVER a week now. He had not come to grips with his changed status; far from it. But he could cope. There were times when he wandered off in daytime dreaming; when the past—twenty years gone in fact, but only last week for Dave—seemed more real than this fantasy present. But he could cope, and a truer accommodation would come with time. It was not, he told himself, as if he had been completely unprepared for this. All his life he had worked toward making physiological resurrection a reality.

But twenty years! He hadn't counted on that.

There were other things he hadn't counted on. That Shashi had come to hate him during the last days of his other life—days he could never know. The Dave Singer who had died had been a subtly different person than he was. That Dave had experienced several crucial weeks of life that this Dave had missed, and had been changed by them. Dave knew of those weeks, of course, but only secondhand. Since the experience was not truly his, he could not react to it as that Dave would have.

It bothered him immensely.

It had taken four days before he could even remain awake a full ten hours in succession, but there was basically nothing wrong with his body except that it had never known the stress of gravity and exercise. For the second half of his first week he had worked at isometric exercises, and now, on the ninth day of his "life," Dave was able to sit in a wheelchair. He also got his first look at a mirror, and the pasty, emaciated image that stared back sickened him. He vowed then to make his body over into the image of an athlete. Before he had given little thought to his body; it had been reasonably well developed from hard labor during his boyhood, and his appetites as a man had not been excessive. It had served him well.

Now he was suddenly transformed into an invalid and he found his body's true worth.

He discussed diet and exercise with Angelena. She was a nurse, though it had been years since she had had the opportunity to practice. She was a petite, wiry woman, a natural athlete, and this had left her looking ten years younger than her fifty years. She had brought him a light set of weights and he was sitting in the sun, darkening his skin and building up his strength, when Jim Brighan came to warn him of Shashi's coming.

Shashi and Nirghaz were living together and raising Dave's clonechild. They had been together since Dave's death, but Shashi had broken with Dave before that. So Dave had been told, although he did not know the details. There had been a widening rift at the time of his last taping, so he was not entirely surprised.

Shashi had refused to have any part of the project. That fitted with her earlier attitude. Apparently, she had caused trouble when Nirghaz donated the cell sample that had led to Dave's resurrection. That he did not understand, nor did he understand why Nirghaz had nothing to do with the project. Surely he, of all people, would consider it indispensable.

They had raised Dave's cloneson. His name was Chandra Ayyar; Ayyar was the name Shashi and Nirghaz had taken as their masquerade during the years they were hunted by the Secret Police. Chandra was nineteen and in college at Poona.

Dave had steeled himself for this meeting. The difference between age twenty-four and age forty-five would have wrought changes in her infinitely greater than the changes in Jim Brigham. And Brigham had never been Dave's lover.

She entered the compound with Angelena, and Dave had a minute to study her as she walked across the grass. Her waist was still trim and her hips and breasts full. She weighed perhaps a few kilograms more, but it had not ruined her figure. Her face had always run more toward serenity than vivacity. Only rarely, usually during lovemaking, did she giggle like a young girl. Now her age had caught up to her attitude and she seemed all in proportion: a calm, handsome woman who was still desirable.

But there were wrinkles around her eyes that time hadn't put there, and she looked as if she didn't smile enough anymore.

"Hello, Shashi."

"Hello."

"I missed you. You should have come sooner."

She licked her lips, looking trapped. He wondered if she was embarrassed by her liaison with Nirghaz and hoped that that was all that stood between them. It was not.

"I came only to discharge one last debt."

"Shashi, nothing I remember and nothing anyone has told me about our time together at the end justifies your hatred of me. I know that we had hard times at the end, though I don't remember them, but were they so bad as to cause this?"

"I don't hate you."

"You seem to."

"I just don't know who you are."

"I am David Singer. Or Ram David Singh, if you prefer that name."

"No, you aren't."

"Hell, Shashi, forget the shell. You aren't looking at a fifteen-year-old boy. You were with Nirghaz during his recovery, so you shouldn't react like this."

"Your looks don't have anything to do with my reactions. Give me more credit than that."

He was silenced by her attitude, more than by her words. He had not dreamed that this much of a gap could have sprung up between them.

"Did anyone tell you what happened to me when Ramadav died?"

"No," he replied. "What happened when *I* died?"

"When Ramadav died, his *atman* entered the child in my womb."

"Nonsense."

She turned angrily. "Nonsense? How would you know? I was there; I felt it. I *know!*"

"And I am here. I am myself, fully; *I* know it."

She almost smiled then, but her tears ruined it. Very softly, she said, "Well, at least you sound like him."

He scowled and turned his head away. He had not looked forward to this meeting, but now it was as if the intervening twenty years had not happened. The old familiar arguments were still there and their basic incompatibility lay between them. It angered him, and it saddened him.

She went on. "But you aren't that person. That which was Ram David Singh transmigrated to my child. That which was the essence of the man I loved now resides in Chandra, ready and willing to experience life again, fresh and untainted. No mere rerun of old experiences, old mistakes. That's why I'm staying away from the project—that and my repugnance at the whole thing. I intend Chandra to have a chance at a new life."

Dave could only stare. The idea was so foreign to his

thinking that he could not take it seriously. He snorted and shook his head. "And me? If that is true, what am I?"

"I don't know."

"I do. I am David Singer and you are out of your mind."

"So you think."

"So I know."

She let it drop without conceding anything. The heat of the sun, heretofore welcome, had become oppressive. Like this conversation. It didn't seem to be leading anywhere, and Dave could feel his hold on his temper slipping as his fatigue grew.

"If what you say is true," he said, "why come to me? What am I to you?"

She looked at him long and sadly. "You are a phantom out of my past. You are a walking dead man. You are an abomination—and yet, I hunger at the sight of your face."

"I still love you."

"Shut up!"

"I do."

Tears were flowing freely down her face, but she remained unchanged.

"Shashi, what did you come here for?"

"To ask you, in memory of the man who once wore that sweet body, in the name of the man you think yourself to be, to leave me and mine utterly alone. Never to seek me out. Never to contact my son. Not to haunt me like the ghost that you are."

"My God, Shashi! Do you know what you're asking? He's my son, too."

"You had no hand in raising him. You have no right to see him."

"That was not my fault."

"Stop!" she screamed, then fought to control her voice. "Stop it! Stop talking as if you were Ramadav."

"I am."

She balled her fists until they trembled, but there was no vent for her frustration.

"Dammit, Shashi! You accept Nirghaz. Why not me?"

She could not answer. Her face was twisted into a mask of hatred. There was no lesser term for the emotion. Tears streamed unchecked and she could find no words. She turned away and stumbled once as she began to walk toward the gate.

"You haven't told Chandra about me, have you?"

Dave's voice was mild, but it nailed her where she stood. She turned back momentarily. "No. And you must not tell him. I forbid it."

"I will, you know."

She stood for a moment, uncertain, beaten. Then she turned and ran toward the gate.

Chapter 22

DAVE SHOVED THE WALKER FORWARD A few centimeters and shuffled a step to catch up, repeated the motion, then rested momentarily. His wheelchair sat twenty meters behind him; it had taken him five minutes to cover that distance, but he was happy with his progress. Ten days out of his metal womb and he was walking for the first time. Joyne, Angelena's and Anson's daughter, was with him. She hovered nearby to steady him, but that hadn't been necessary so far. Although, Dave thought, it might not be a bad idea to totter just enough to get her arms around him. She was just past twenty and looked much as her mother must have looked at that age. Dave's mind was mature, but his rapidly strengthening body was pumping young hormones that sent his imagination wandering.

He shuffled forward again. He had set fifty meters as a goal and he did not intend to be deterred. His ten days as an invalid was driving him up the wall, and he intended to push his recovery as hard as possible. There were a lot of things he wanted to do. That thought sent his glance back to Joyne again.

She smiled and said, "You look like you feel good."

He didn't answer at once. His sorrow at Shashi's attitude had been short lived. They were far along the road to desperation when he made his last taping, and their brief meeting had reminded him forcibly of the worst aspects of their life together. It made her easier to forget.

"Yes, Joyne—happier than I can remember being in a long time."

She looked puzzled. He realized that for her he had just come to exist, while his experiences were an unbroken chain without even a heartbeat's gap between his last taping and his reawakening. She realized it, too, and they shared a smile at their congruent thoughts before she said, "Even though I grew up with the concept of immortality, and knew that you would be a thirty-five-year-old man in a fifteen-year-old's body, I still find it hard to relate to you. You are a legend in the family, and yet . . ."

"Family?" he interrupted.

"That's what Dad and Mum and the others call themselves. We've lived together for almost twenty years as a group; I was only two when Uncle Jim found Mum and Dad, and the family is the only life I've known.

"I grew up with tales of you and your research, and once, when I was a little girl, I saw the lifetapes you had sent Uncle Jim. I had nightmares for years after, thinking that all you were was wrapped up in those spools. It was so strange. Now it seems normal."

"Good for you. It doesn't seem normal to me, even now."

"I guess you have to grow up with it."

"Yeah."

He concentrated on walking then, suddenly aware of the great gap between their ages and experiences. His sexual awareness was even dulled for a time, but that soon changed as he became aware again that the fashions of this latter day had led her to wear a thin shirt that let the darkness of her nipples show clearly through. She seemed unaware of this; and probably she was, for it was the norm of the day. Angelena and Julia Villanova dressed the same way.

But twenty years ago real time, or a week ago by Dave's emotional reckoning, breasts had not been casually displayed. He felt a swelling in his groin and clenched his teeth in frustration that he could not control it. That was one of the embarrassments of adolescence that had come back to haunt him, and he was too old in his mind to take it with good grace.

To cover his embarrassment, he shifted his path and let himself carefully down onto a bench. Joyne swung the walker away and sat beside him. He was acutely conscious of her presence. *Damn*, he groaned inwardly, *I had forgotten how a young boy can burn*.

"You seem to be progressing rapidly. Mum is amazed."

Dave nodded. "It's a matter of dedication—making up your mind to ignore the pain. Actually, it's easier to be brave and push, because if the recovery period is going to be painful anyway, it might as well be short.

"Coming to terms with my body is the easy part. It's that missing twenty years that is going to be tough to deal with. I'm going to have to do a lot of learning before I leave here or I won't even be able to make my way around on the outside without having half the people I meet think I'm crazy."

She giggled. "You'll have to learn to talk all over again. You wouldn't believe some of the outdated slang you've been using."

"Oh, I hadn't thought of that. Correct me when I goof, please."

"Okay."

"I've been watching the holo and reading all the newstats I can lay hands on, but things still don't always seem to come together. Everything I see or read assumes a body of shared experience. I will have to depend on the rest of you to help fill me in."

"Have you tried encyclopedia yearbooks? Start with the year of your . . ." She chopped her phrase off in mid-sentence.

"Death?"

She flushed and nodded. Her sudden shyness was at such odds with her usual brashness that it caused Dave to smile. "Don't be embarrassed. I died. It means nothing, as long as I am alive again now."

She swallowed, thinking of the rows of cylindrical lifetapes Jim Brigham had so carefully guarded through the decades, and of the nightmares they had caused her. "I'm sorry. It wasn't something I meant to bring up."

"Forget it. *I* never died, because I don't remember it. *I* went directly from a taping session to here with no consciousness of intervening time, so what happened after my last taping is just so much fantasy as far as any emotional reaction I might have."

She merely shrugged and said, "Your death was real to me."

"What were you saying?" Dave asked, trying to steer the conversation back onto a reasonably even track. "Yearbooks?"

"Oh. I thought you might get the encyclopedia yearbooks starting with the year you . . . died . . . and skim them one year at a time so that you build up a picture of today chronologically."

"That sounds like a good idea."

Dave reached for his walker and Joyne nudged it into his reach but did not offer to help him rise. She was a girl of surprising sensitivity; no, not so surprising if you considered her as her mother's daughter. Dave dragged himself up, trying unsuccessfully to suppress a groan. She offered no sympathy; he appreciated that. Quite a nice girl, really; he mentally changed the subject to avoid another erection. That was one adolescent physical reaction he intended to bring under control immediately.

There was a time and place for everything, for God's sake!

She walked with him, but less closely now. Obviously, she did not think he was likely to fall.

"What happened between you and Shashi?" Joyne asked. "She certainly left here in a hurry the other day." When Davé didn't answer, she glanced up to see his face set in hard lines. "What's wrong?" she asked suddenly.

"What happened between Shashi and me was personal and private."

"Well, excuse me!" she snapped. "I know you were lovers, but that was twenty years ago."

Then she slapped her hands over her mouth, suddenly aware of her *faux pas*.

"Not for me, it wasn't," Dave replied, and the gap in their years yawned between them.

That night, all the light went out in Dave's world. Even as his happiness had seemed misplaced in the midst of his pain, this black depression seemed to spring from nowhere. It came on him in a matter of minutes, between supper and sleeping.

Anson saw it first and called for his wife. The whole household had been on the lookout for this reaction; Nirghaz had warned them to expect it. Angelena gave him a mild sedative and sat through the night with him, in case he should awaken unexpectedly.

And that night Joyne had nightmares about a man's life sealed up in metal spools.

Chapter 23

THE DEPRESSION PASSED IN THE NIGHT, but left Dave feeling languid. He forced himself to do his fifty meters and even walked a little way without the walker, but did not push himself further.

Nirghaz came in the afternoon. Dave was lying back absorbing the late spring sunshine, and as he watched Nirghaz cross the yard he felt a pride grow up in him like nothing he had ever felt before.

Nirghaz was walking.

When Dave had seen him last he had been a legless cripple; though Dave knew secondhand that he had succeeded in giving Nirghaz back his legs, the impact of it had not hit him until now.

It was as if his whole life was vindicated by that one act.

Nirghaz was older, of course, but the resurrection process had thrown his biological age back, just as it had so recently done to Dave, so that Nirghaz was apparently in his mid-thirties.

Nirghaz's smile grew lopsided as he approached, and broke into a grin. He ran the last few meters and Dave

145

met him with open arms, grasping him around the waist and hugging him close in a display of affection that surprised them both.

"My God, it's good to see you, Nirghaz. And walking." Dave pushed him to arm's length, looked him up and down, and just grinned.

"It *is* a miracle. I've been walking for twenty years, but I'll never forget what it was like before, nor ever stop being thankful to you."

Dave waved that aside. "I wasn't fishing for that; we did it together."

Nirghaz pulled up a chair and sat beside Dave while Dave tripped the chaise into an upright position. "You're looking good," Nirghaz said.

"Hell, I look like something that crawled up out of a grave. But at least I'm losing that dead-fish whiteness, and look at this." He held up his arm and flexed his biceps. "That may look like nothing to you, but that's twice the meat I had there a week ago."

"You've changed. You were never this carefree before."

Dave sobered momentarily, then grinned again. "Why shouldn't I be happy? The resurrection process works. And no matter how hard I tried to believe in my own work before, there was always a doubt. My Millennialist upbringing kept saying, 'You are tampering with things you have no right to control.' Now that I know that the process works, that burden is lifted."

The conversation veered then to the project, to what had been done in the last few days, and to family gossip regarding Anson, Joyne, Jim, and the others. It was clear to Dave that after the first open exchange of affection, a wall had quickly grown up between them. There was something that Nirghaz did not want to discuss.

So he cut Nirghaz off. "Forget that, Nirghaz. I'm not interested. Something is bothering you, so spit it out."

Nirghaz dropped the small talk, but was clearly at a loss as to how to phrase what was on his mind. In a moment of clairvoyance, Dave added, "It's Shashi, isn't it?"

Nirghaz nodded. "I didn't know how you would greet me, Ramadav. I expected you to be jealous of our living together, since by your timeline you two were lovers only days ago."

"And now you're disappointed because I'm not?"

"Of course not! But I was so keyed up for a confrontation that it colors my reactions." His fingers drummed the chair momentarily, before he added, "Dammit, Ramadav, why aren't you jealous? I don't understand you."

The question deserved a serious and honest reply. Dave carefully marshaled his thoughts before saying, "My relationship with Shashi was going downhill already at the time of my last taping. That accounts for part of my attitude. Also, the shock of being reborn twenty years out of time with a weeks-long segment of my life forever erased has made this like no other period. It allows for rapid changes—no, *demands* them.

"Look at me, fifteen years old, for God's sake. My penis pops to attention every time Joyne walks by. It's a wonder I don't wet myself—probably I did during the first few days and I just don't remember it. And you. You're fifteen years older than when I last saw you, and walking. And at that you've changed less than Jim or Shashi.

"But part of it is Shashi herself. Did she talk about what happened between us here?"

"She wouldn't, even though I asked."

"She thinks that my *atman* transmigrated at my death to our clonechild. She thinks I'm some kind of a zombie, and won't acknowledge that I am David Singer at all."

Nirghaz considered that momentarily. "I knew how she felt about Chandra. And I had some idea how she felt about you—that is, in your present incarnation. We had the worst fight of a relatively stormy twenty years over whether or not I should provide the cell sample for your present body, and she still hasn't forgiven me for going ahead against her wishes."

"I'm sorry things aren't better for the two of you."

"So am I, but don't blame yourself. The basic problem is that the project is the most important thing in my life. I have maintained only tenuous contact with it for twenty years for her sake, but she isn't satisfied. She wants me to make a complete break and she can't understand that I won't." He looked up at Dave with weariness and bitterness in his eyes. "She wants me to commit suicide, but she doesn't see it that way."

Dave merely reached out to take Nirghaz's hand. When he had inherited Shashi, he had also inherited all of Dave's difficulties in dealing with her viewpoints. Dave had no advice to offer; he had not been able to handle the problem himself, so he changed the subject.

"Tell me about Chandra. I know his name and his age, but not much else."

Nirghaz smiled with fatherly pride and this time Dave did feel jealousy. "Chandra looks just like you. Stupid thing to say, really, since he was cloned from your old body and your present body from his."

For the first time, Dave realized that Chandra was his father, as well as his son. The thought held disquieting resonances, but he put it away. It was a pseudo-paradox brought on by the inadequacies of old kinship terminology in the face of new techniques.

Still, it bothered him.

"Chandra is Indian in his outlook. He lacks your brashness and informality. He acts much as you would expect a child of Shashi's to act—quiet and refined, a very giving child. He was a pleasure to raise.

"He is away at college in Poona now."

"What does he think of the project? Joyne has been trying to show me what it was like for her to grow up with the possibility of immortality as a real part of her world."

"Chandra doesn't know."

"What! What do you mean, he doesn't know? You have him on lifetapes, don't you?"

"No. Shashi . . ."

Dave sat bolt upright, anger darkening his face. "What in hell do you mean by this? By what right do you deny my son his birthright? I want him told, and I mean now. And I want him on lifetapes. If you don't do it, I will. My God, Nirghaz, he could die tomorrow; youth is no shield against death."

Nirghaz cringed. He had never seen Dave really angry before, and he was more than a little shamed by his own position. A thousand times he had argued with Shashi, but he had never brought things to a head by going against her wishes and telling Chandra, anyway. Because of Chandra's youth and good health he had put it off, knowing that that was the break that might destroy their relationship entirely.

He tried to explain some of this, but Dave simply snarled, "Shashi be damned!"

The angry silence continued between them for some minutes until Dave forced himself to say, "Nirghaz, I understand how it is. I know why you put this off, because I know Shashi. But you must not put it off any longer. You may think that I am overcautious because I so recently 'died', but death is no respecter of age. I love you, Nirghaz. You and Jim are the truest friends I have. I will not have you hating yourself because you put off telling Chandra until it was too late."

"You're right, of course."

"Come on, now," Dave said, forcing a smile. "Let's change the subject. Tell me about you and Shashi. What are your lives like now?"

Chapter 24

EACH FOOTFALL SENT A VIBRATION UP Dave's legs to jar the base of his spine, and his spine transmitted that force upward into his already booming head. With each footfall his forearm shot forward across his belly, then was snatched back as his balance changed. Those forearms were thicker now, though still lean; he drew sweet air deeply into his lungs.

He turned at the wall of the compound and raced across the grass. The aching in his chest worsened, but he ignored it. Another turn and he was running back toward the patio. His breath was groaning in and out now, but he persisted to cross the invisible goal line he had set for himself. He turned about in a stumbling walk that let his sweating body cool, then flopped onto the grass, testing his pulse to see how quickly it would drop.

In five minutes the first flush of exhaustion had passed, and in ten he rose and went in to breakfast.

Anson was there just finishing a melon. Dave sat beside him and began filling his plate. Rashers of bacon followed rolls, eggs, jam, a bowl of hot cereal, and a melon of his own. Anson chuckled and Dave raised his juice glass in a half-salute. "Growing boy, you know," he said, grinning.

"I guess! How far did you run today?"

"Half a kilometer. I want to get up to ten kilometers, four times a week, and level off there. That's what I ran in college before my work at the Institute started taking up all my time."

Anson watched as Dave dug into the meal. He searched for just the right phrase to describe the change that had taken place in the month since Dave's resurrection. The increased girth of his limbs and chest he discounted. These were evident, but were not the essence of the change. Then he had it; Dave's body had begun to look lived in. The smoothness of his face had gone. Wrinkles had begun to form in conformance with his customary expressions: tiny crow's feet at the outer edges of his eyes, hollows beside the nose which reformed themselves each time he grinned, and twin vertical slashes between his brows that formed each time he squinted in concentration.

Anson had not spent much time with Dave in the last month; he was nearing the completion of his latest innovation, a computer-balanced neural cancellation device that would eventually let them grow sensory-deprived clones outside S.D. tanks. Those could be exercised before they were quickened to avoid this miserable period of conditioning.

"Dave," he said, "there is one thing I don't understand. I know that training your body takes time, but I am still surprised that you aren't already back in the harness."

"You mean doing research?"

"Yes."

"Well," Dave said, "I will certainly do something to earn my keep eventually, but first I have to re-educate myself."

"Now, wait a minute. I didn't mean to imply that you are leeching. If you never did another thing, *Inquiry* would justify your entire future existence. I just meant that if I were you, I would be spending every spare minute in the labs. Your research opened up new vistas, but you don't seem very interested in them."

"I'm not."

"Eh? That doesn't make sense."

Dave pushed away his plate, now fifteen hundred calories emptier, and sipped his coffee. "Anson, I'm not a scientist. Never was. That is, I am not motivated by what motivates you and the other professionals. The only thing I was ever looking for was an avoidance of dying.

"Now, I know Shashi is still doing barrenness research, and I know that the government is growing ten thousand 'ideal' clonechildren a year, and that Sindhara has developed a mutant strain of rye that is resistant to low-level radiation. That all fascinates me—as a concerned human being. But to do research in any of those fields—no way."

Anson shrugged. "I guess after *Inquiry,* anything else would be an anticlimax."

Dave began to gather up his soiled dishes and Anson joined him. "I'll stop in to see your research soon, Anson, and everyone else's. But right now I have my hands full trying to get a feeling for the year 2223. I have a whole new world to explore out there, and a whole lot of thinking to do about the philosophical implications of what we have done."

"I thought that was all clear in your mind before you started."

"Hardly."

Joyne's idea of using yearbooks was a good one; through them Dave began to get a picture of his new world.

There had been changes in twenty years. No one had found a cure for barrenness, but five years earlier the government of India had set out to find the thousand most perfect genotypes to be replicated. For months the newstats carried little else. Tests were prepared, disputed, denounced, praised, and ultimately carried out. Statistics showed incontrovertibly that Dravidian stock was underrepresented and there were no individuals selected from those few tribals who remained, but at least none of those selected was in any way defective. Now each month brought a new clone fetus from each donor to be implanted in some Indian woman. Twelve thousand new births each year. This was the fourth year of the project and there were those who wanted it expanded faster, or more cautiously, or stopped altogether.

Styles had changed. In the last five years, two generations of emphasis on motherhood and the difference between the sexes had gone under, and unisex clothing was the order of the day. For twenty years women had chosen new ways of covering their breasts to emphasize them; now they were baring them casually and the emphasis had shifted to the midriff.

Sri Karji had held his party together for fifteen years, but in the two decades since his death the balance of power in Parliament had shifted eight times. Fifteen years after Bhargava's ignominious departure, scandal consciousness was still rampant.

The Ganga project had drained most of the Ganges basin. The Peace of Mahmet had brought a cessation of warfare between Medina and India after the Nehru had made Medinan retaliation a theoretical impossibility. Then the Medinans had built a force beam in secret and had blown the Nehru out of the sky. Negotiations were under way again, and war or peace was imminent, depending on which newstat one read. Meanwhile, Indians and Medinans continued to gleefully destroy one another on the now dry plains of the Panch-ab.

The year 2223 was, in short, a year much like any other.

Joyne had invited Dave to a picnic in the hills above the compound. She was supplying his clothing so that he would become accustomed to wearing what was currently stylish in the world outside. Today she had chosen for him a pair of skintight trousers, cut low across the hips, and a short, open vest. Her outfit was the same, and each carried a waist pack. His standards of beauty and desirability were two decades out of joint, so he was acutely aware of her bare breasts and thankful that he had finally mastered his erotic reflexes.

For Joyne it had been a strained month. She had grown up with tales of Ram David Singh and his research and had read *Inquiry* as soon as she was able to understand the concepts. She had thought of him a little like a folk hero. To see him reincarnated in the body of a fifteen-year-old boy was difficult.

Yet in that month his personality had taken command. His face had aged at least ten years and his body was filling out fast. In another month he would pass for twenty-five.

Her eyes saw a youth, but his patterns of speech, his references, and the subjects he chose to talk about were discomfortingly at odds with his features, and she often missed the significance of what he was saying because the references he made were keyed to a world that had ended twenty years ago.

Joyne led out, following the service road out of the compound until it was cut by a footpath. The compound had once been the summer retreat of a minor raja and after that a hill station where British civil servants went to wait out the enervating heat that preceded the monsoon. It was an area of dry, open jungle above fifteen hundred meters in elevation. The Mahanadi flowed somewhere to the north.

The path wound upward and doubled back to a point overlooking the compound. Dave could see the neat rows of bungalows and the massive central palace surrounded by formal gardens. The gardens were in considerable disrepair now, since it was the policy of the family to restrict outsiders from the compound.

Angelena had taken it upon herself to preserve them somewhat, and he could see her at work now.

They walked for two hours, crossing the hill on which the compound rested, then dropping down into the dry valley beyond and following a mostly dry watercourse upward to a place where it had formed a series of small pools. There they spread out their meal and ate.

Afterward, Dave drew Joyne into relating more of her girlhood. She told him of the constant traveling and ever-present danger of having their masquerade penetrated. She had felt only some of the horror of that refugee existence, but Dave could extrapolate to what Anson and Angelena had felt. He found himself becoming angry all over again at Bhatt, whom he had thought harmless, and Bhargava, whom he had never met.

After a while they tired of lying in the sun and waded. The water was cool, but thick with algae. Joyne slipped on the slimy bottom and managed, not accidentally, to tumble Dave with her. They emerged sputtering and splashing each other. Her open vest was plastered to her sides and her wet breasts glinted in the sun. Dave's heart beat a tattoo in his groin and this time he could not control the swelling. She saw and desisted, but later when they lay down in the sun to dry themselves, she pillowed her head on his arm.

Then she led him to tell of his own past and he recounted the joys of his Ozark childhood, all going sour when he rejected his natal religion. She was all wide-eyed interest through this, but later when he spoke more casually of the Institute, of Shashi, Nirghaz, Gopal, and Sri Karji, she became cold and distant.

She began to pack the debris of their lunch, and when he asked her what the matter was, she would not reply.

Chapter 25

A COLD GREETING AWAITED NIRGHAZ IN Raipur. Shashi was finishing supper when he came in. He shouted a greeting toward the kitchen. She did not answer.

It was an old routine. Whenever he went up to the compound, which was not often, he took the monorail, leaving in the morning and returning the same evening. He never stayed overnight; it was as if that would have been betraying a trust. When he returned she always had supper ready and they would spend the evening in quiet formality. It would take a week or more before the routine of normal living dispelled the ghosts his trips raised.

Nirghaz thought of it as marriage, although the name they shared was fictitious and neither state nor church had recognized the liaison. It was the intention for permanence that counted.

In the early years they had discussed the resurrection process, but now they slid past the subject as gracefullas they could. There was no point in further discussion, still less in argument; they were both too firmly grounded in their opinions.

She was waiting for him when he returned to the kitchen. She spooned out a plate of curry for him, then one for herself and sat down across from him. He could see that she had been crying.

He stared down at the plate, then pushed it away. "Shashi, about Chandra . . ."

She knew what was coming; he could see it in her stiff motions. "What about Chandra?"

"We have to tell him about the project."

"No."

Her last word; her only word. But this time it seemed less sure than merely tired.

"Shashi, he has a right to decide his life for himself."

That's not for you to say; if you wish, that's not for me to say, either. Ram's words, coming back from across the gap of two decades to haunt her. Like the *thing* that Nirghaz and the others had created. Her face twisted with anger and she slammed her fork down.

For a long moment their eyes locked, love dying down before the onslaught of anger.

Shashi could see that this argument would be different. Nirghaz had found an ally in Dave's zombie. Now he would have the courage to go against her will, and she was defenseless.

Since Chandra was an infant she had known that the time would come when Nirghaz would tell him of the project, just as she knew that the day would come when Nirghaz would leave her.

Some women age gracefully and evenly. Others hold on to their youths far past all reason, and when middle age comes to them, it swoops in all at once. Shashi was one of these.

Some morning she would wake up to find her hair gone gray and her figure failing. That did not trouble her in itself. Vanity had never been one of her weaknesses. But when her age tumbled in upon her, Nirghaz would leave. Perhaps not at once, but as surely as night follows day.

Nirghaz was still speaking. "Dave told me what went on between the two of you the other day. Why did you do that to him?"

"Ram David Singh is dead. That creature up there is not him."

Nirghaz refrained from arguing. Chandra carried the *atman* of Ram David Singh; Shashi had said it, and for her it was incontrovertible. Sometimes he was jealous of Chandra for that, thinking he saw that belief reflected in her actions. He had challenged her on it once. He would not do so now. The hurt in her eyes had closed that avenue of communication forever.

"I spent two hours with him today, Shashi. It's Ramadav, as surely as I am myself."

She flashed a startled look and quickly hid it. What had he seen in her eyes—doubt of *his* identity? After twenty years together, could she still have that waking nightmare that he was some kind of demon? Even if it were so, she would deny it.

"Have it your own way," she said. "It means nothing one way or the other."

Oh, but it does.

"Shashi, we owe it to Chandra to let him make up his own mind on this."

"So why tell me about it? You've obviously made up your mind already. Between you and that *thing,* I don't stand a chance."

"Dave said . . ." He stopped, but the damage was done. *Hell with it,* he thought, and went on. "Dave pointed out something I really already knew. Death is not restricted to the old. I just can't put this off any longer."

"So you've finally found the courage to do it."

She said it to hurt him, and it did, deeply. But it also angered him, because of all the times he had come so close to telling Chandra and had held back because he didn't want to hurt Shashi. He said, "Yes!", because nothing else needed to be said, and nothing else would have hurt her more.

She tried to remain calm. "Will you at least wait a while? Give him time to grow, to mature. He is too young still to know his own mind and too young for the masquerade."

"What do you mean?"

"Dammit, Nirghaz, don't you ever miss your childhood and your old friends?"

He only shrugged. She knew that he did not. His childhood had been miserable and his friends few. Sri Karji he missed, and Srinivas, but both were dead now.

"You're cold, Nirghaz; cold as a fish. You don't even know what I'm talking about, do you? We've lived here for ten years and I don't have one person I can take into my confidence and really call a friend. Not one! How could I? How could I tell them about my family, or my childhood, or where I've been or what I've done? Or what I've dreamed?

"Nirghaz, I stopped being Shashi Mathur the day we went underground. I lost all my life up to that point because if you have to deny it, it dries up and blows away. I have to deny it every day and be Shashi Ayyar; and who is *she?* She hasn't any life at all, just a bungalow and a one-room lab. No friends, no visitors, no intercourse with the world beyond these walls. Because any indiscretion might set us on the run again."

Shashi broke down momentarily, and wiped her eyes angrily. "Is that what you want for Chandra? Because the moment he knows about the project, he can no longer live an unguarded life.

"It isn't just the resurrection process. God knows I hate it and don't want Chandra sucked into it, but that isn't all. I don't want him to live like we've had to live. Not so young. He deserves better than that."

"I don't want my son to die," Nirghaz said.

"Oh, Nirghaz, is that the worst fate in the world?"

He looked sadly at her and said the one word that stood like a wall between them. "Yes."

And this time he was too far committed to be swayed. He pitied her, but he did not reach out to touch her.

"Just a little time at least, Nirghaz. Just a little more time before you tear his world apart. Please; is that too much to ask?"

"Yes, Shashi, it is too much."

Chandra Ayyar took a jet from Bombay to Ranchi and then the monorail to Raipur. Nirghaz was waiting for him at the station, but his mother was not there. A momentary fear shot through him. His father's letter had asked for his immediate return, and all the subsequent assurances that no one he knew was hurt or ill could not stop him from speculating. Exams were near and his father would not have called him back for some trivial reason.

Nirghaz avoided his questions as he drove up into the hills above the city. The sun was setting as they settled in side by side on a grassy knoll.

How to start? *Son, have you ever thought about immortality?* Stupid; oblique and stupid. Better to be as direct as possible.

"Chandra, did you ever hear of Ram David Singh?"

Even in the near darkness, Nirghaz could feel the cool mantle of caution slipping over Chandra, and he wished that they could have been closer. But how can you be close to a boy when all the experiences of your own childhood have to be edited to fit the masquerade you hold up even before him?

"Yes."

That surprised Nirghaz. He had thought that Dave was forgotten. "Did you ever hear of a paper called *Inquiry into Artificially Induced Immortality?*"

When Chandra replied, his tone was carefully non-committal. "Yes."

Two surprises; perhaps this would be easier than Nirghaz had anticipated. "Have you read it?"

This time Chandra didn't reply at all, and Nirghaz took the absence of a negative as a yes. Then Chandra said, "You know how it is in college. The underground presses are always grinding out something. Usually it is a political tract. Sometimes you can even pick them up out of the litter in the streets and never know where they come from."

I don't know how it got into my pocket, Dad. Honest! Nirghaz chuckled in relief and real amusement. "Chandra, would it make this conversation any easier for you if I told you that I had read *Inquiry* and that I approve of it?"

"I suppose," Chandra said, but he didn't sound relieved.

Chandra had always been an enigma for Nirghaz. Perhaps he should have spent more time with him, but there had always been demands. First they had to dodge the Secret Police and later try to establish some kind of home. And the masquerade had always been there.

Depending on Chandra's youthful resilience, Nirghaz wasted no more time on preliminaries. "Ram David Singh, or David Singer, was a North American who came to India to work. He was a friend of mine and of your mother. After his death, your mother and I were hounded for a number of years by the Secret Police. When Bhargava was deposed the pressure let up and we have been able to stay unmolested since then by keeping a low profile and taking new names."

Nirghaz paused to see what effect his words were having. Chandra did not look at him; he was staring hard toward the still ruddy western sky and Nirghaz could see him swallow heavily. Finally, Chandra chuckled bitterly, "All my life I knew I was different. Other children had uncles and grandparents and fitted into a life much larger than themselves. I always felt like a *pariha* because I had only you and Mother, and neither of you would ever talk about your pasts."

It was very Indian, Nirghaz thought, for Chandra to need to know where he stood in a web of kinship.

"Who were you before you went underground?"

"Your mother's real name is Shashi Mathur. She was a scientist at the I.A.B.R. when I met her. I never knew her family, and you will have to ask her for details on that. I was Nirghaz Husain, son of Parivar Husain and Usha Kantikar. My grandfather was Jogendranath Kantikar."

"Sri Karji!"

"Yes."

Chandra struggled with shock, trying to bring together his schoolboy knowledge of the history of two decades past. "But Nirghaz Husain was supposed to have been crippled in the bombing of Mahmet—he lost his legs."

"Yes."

"But . . ." He couldn't bring his confusion into a coherent question.

"I lost my legs and later regained them by memory taping and resurrection."

"Krishna! No, you can't be telling me the truth. What . . ." He trailed off, shaking his head. Nirghaz took pity on him and remained silent, watching the sky grow dark and the stars wink into view. A warm, dry wind caressed the two of them and the only sounds were cicadas and the munching of cattle.

Chapter 26

DAVE FOUND JIM BRIGHAM SPRAWLED loosely on the grass in the garden watching the constellations. He patted the ground beside him and Dave dropped into lotus position, feeling a curious rapport between them. To an observer, they were youth and age. That was illusion; yet in the midst of illusion was a thread of truth, for Jim Brigham had wisdom born of an understanding of his fellowmen beyond any Dave would ever possess, even as Dave's brilliance outshown Jim.

Jim Brigham was old. Dave didn't know his exact age, but he had to be in his seventies. He was lean and healthy—in much better health than he had been twenty-five years ago, in fact. His flight and renewed interest in life accounted for that. Nevertheless, he did not stir himself beyond the compound and he tired easily.

Now he had decided to renew. Tomorrow he would enter an S.D. tank for his final taping and emerge with his persona imprinted on a young clone.

Jim lay quietly communing with the universe of lights

against darkness that displayed itself in a slow-moving panorama before him, and eventually Dave felt some of the quietness and peace of the man flow into him, slowing his heartbeat and stilling his breathing. Jim reached out to touch him at the elbow and from his withered fingers Dave felt a current flow through him, heating and cooling him at once. He was reminded of something but the exact referent was lost in time. Slowly Jim's hand came down his forearm until their hands clasped like lovers. No; the communication here was asexual and much deeper than that. It was . . . ; but, no, there were no words. The hand in his was both a challenge and a comfort, and in that fusing of opposites Dave knew the nagging memory for what it was. For one brief moment he felt again the fearful sureness, the unfettered knowing that transcended mundane knowledge which he had felt on that day when his old religion had given way to an awareness of the inevitability of death.

The moment passed. Jim withdrew his hand and the dark masses of vegetation that occluded a part of the sky were merely trees and bushes again. They no longer merged into a wholeness that encompassed Dave and Jim, the undergirding earth and the overarching sky.

Orion had marched an hour further on his journey across the sky. Dave shook himself as if waking from a dream as he realized the time that had passed and Jim chuckled in harmony with him. Then Jim became silent again for a moment before saying, "You are troubled."

Dave unknotted his legs and rolled over with his back to the sky. The earth beneath his face was fragrant as he laid his cheek against the roughness of newly mowed grass, drinking in the smell of the earth. He was no longer the brash and certain person that he had been. Nirghaz and Shashi had burst his materialism through, not with logic, but with a calm understanding that there was more to life than he or they could or would ever understand. He had not known until now just how strongly they had influenced him.

"Yes, Jim, I am troubled. But this is not the time to discuss it."

The cicadas were singing a paean to the heavens. Why had he not noticed before how much like sitars they sounded?

"I think it is."

"No. My thoughts are about the project, and I would not like to unsettle you on the eve of your reconstruction."

Jim chuckled in the darkness. "I do not think you could unsettle me tonight. I feel very calm and secure in what I am about to do."

When Dave did not reply, Jim went on: "If anything were to upset me, it would be wondering what you have on your mind."

Dave sighed. "Okay. It isn't that I regret anything I have done or said, or anything that the project has caused. It is just that I feel now that the project is only the first step on a long road and that I am too ignorant, or perhaps I should say too unwise, to see where that road leads or even to choose among alternative branchings along it.

"All my life has been goal directed. In youth my goal was salvation and a Godly life. Then I made knowledge of the world beyond my home my goal, and later, learning in general.

"Somewhere along the line all my earlier goals became one, the avoidance of death. And when I realized what my true goal was, I also realized that all my previous goals had somehow directed me toward this." He paused, searching for the right words. "That is, the goals I had thought I was following were subsumed in the new one and I realized that all my life I had been working toward my ultimate goal without knowing it."

"I understand."

Dave rolled over toward the stars again. "Then I—or another *I* of whom I have no memory—achieved that goal. Here I am, all things accomplished and with no

memory of having accomplished them. Some other *I*
carried my life's ambition through and I [*Oh, damn,
there are no words to explain it!*] do not share in his
triumph because I do not remember it." He ground to a
halt in frustration.

"We haven't the words," Jim said, "to cover the
situation. Our language is bound to time as a unidirec-
tional flow, and to personality as a unitary object,
incapable of division."

"My problem is not language. Language is merely an
inconvenience.

"No, just as my old goals were subsumed in new
ones, I now feel that my search for immortality was
merely a tool toward some higher goal."

"What goal is that?"

"I can't say. I don't understand it yet myself, and I
am too bound by the limitations of speech. To know
myself, I suppose. To know who is the *I* that I speak of
when I talk about myself. That all sounds trite, and I
can't seem to express it any better—at least not yet."

Now Jim did seem troubled. "Are you rejecting the
resurrection process?"

"No! Absolutely not. But I now see that its implications are far beyond anything I dreamed before. You
know the old saw: 'You can never step in the same river
twice.' "

" 'Because the waters of the first river have flowed
away, though it looks the same.' Of course."

"The ancients used that simile to compare to the life
of a man who is different from moment to moment,
though he maintains a continuity with what he has
been. Well, it isn't just philosophical speculation
anymore, because each time we tape ourselves we are
capturing the ghost image of a 'self' that existed at a
particular moment in time and preserving it. Each new
taping updates that ghost, but what we have now is the
potential to bring back those ghosts of the past and
converse with the selves we have been."

"Who would dare! But I see your point."

"Yes, it need not be done to be valid. The fact that it is now possible compels us to consider it. If we can generate multiple selves, each a little removed in time from the other and yet each drawn from the same person, who can set a primacy among them, and where is the *I* which I devoted my life to preserving?"

Jim made no answer.

Orion had fled the sky altogether. It was time to put philosophy aside and go in to sleep. There was much to do tomorrow, and for all that Dave had said, refusing resurrection and embracing death would bring him—or mankind—no closer to an answer. But he regretted bitterly that he had not listened more closely to Shashi and the wisdom she had offered him.

When Dave came in from the garden, Nirghaz had returned to the compound, bringing Chandra with him. Their eyes met in instant recognition and for a moment Dave studied his cloneson.

Physically, he was exactly what Dave was trying to become: smooth limbed, sleek and powerful, of medium height with brown hair and eyes, both several shades too light to be Indian. It was Dave's face, and at the same time, the face of a stranger.

Chandra did not return Dave's smile. He looked disappointed, even cheated, and Dave thought: *He has just been told about me.*

Am I his father or his son? And, of course, the answer was, neither. Dave crossed the room, bringing his hands up into *namaste,* and Chandra reciprocated stiffly.

Suspicion, hostility, anger? Just what mix of emotions was that in Chandra's eyes?

It was going to be a tense evening.

Chapter 27

ANSON WAS AT THE CONSOLE OF THE computer with Dave watching over his shoulder. Angelena and Jim saw to their own share of the details, and Joyne, who had no real part to play, stayed close to Jim. She was silent and constrained. Nirghaz and Chandra watched from the side, conversing softly until Jim drew Nirghaz away into the larger room where the S.D. tanks were kept.

"Dave did not choose to be reconstructed," Jim said when he and Nirghaz were well out of range of the others' hearing. "True, he set up the process and would eventually have used it to cheat death, but he never walked wide-eyed into resurrection knowing that it would mean that at least for a time he would be inhabiting two bodies, and that one of them would be intentionally extinguished. You did."

"It was like going to sleep in one body and waking up in the other. There was no sensation of loss of time or identity."

"Spare me, Nirghaz. I know that. I hoped that,

considering how I am following in your footsteps, you would share some of your prior misgivings with me."

"Why? Are you considering backing out?"

"Oh, no. I enjoy the company of my friends and even being a surrogate grandfather to Joyne, but this old body hurts all the time. I can't think as quickly as I once could, and my memory plays tricks on me. There are things that I would have lost forever if I had not recorded them on lifetapes ten years ago. Actually, what I am saying is that I am getting senile."

"I see. You are being driven to the transfer; so was I. I simply could not stand being a legless, sexless cripple."

"Exactly. Nirghaz, I have a fear. Not only one fear, of course, but one that overshadows all the others; and only you can lay it to rest for me."

"What is that?"

"Fear that some one of my friends will be too emotionally attached to me as I now am to allow this husk to be discarded once I am co-resident in two bodies."

Nirghaz dropped his eyes, not wanting to recognize this confidence and the burden it placed on him. Finally, Jim was forced to continue. "Dave said it last night. If I am co-resident in two bodies simultaneously, which one is *me?* Superstitious drivel, perhaps; probably a false dilemma posed by inadequate language. Still, I don't want to go into this without the assurance that there is someone who has already faced the ultimate implications of this process for himself standing by to see to the destruction of my old body before my new body becomes conscious."

"Dave will see to it."

"Not good enough. Dave doesn't realize it, but he is in the midst of a major identity crisis. I can't trust him to act coldly."

"What can I do?"

"Be ready if anything is needed. I doubt that it will

be, but I must have assurance." Jim Brigham's voice had become urgent, almost pleading. "Will you promise this thing to me?"

"Jim, it is a burden I do not want."

"I know."

"I want to refuse."

Jim dropped his hand on Nirghaz's arm, an intimacy that Nirghaz did not want, and all at once Nirghaz realized: *He really is an old man.* Jim's expression pleaded wordlessly. Nirghaz turned away from that need and asked, "What will you do if I refuse?"

"Stay in this body and grow senile. Nirghaz, looking out of young eyes to see . . . *myself,* still trapped in this old body . . ." He shivered. "It is the only thing I fear more than death."

Nirghaz was subdued when they returned; Jim, on the other hand, was in bubbling good humor. He found it hugely amusing to contemplate himself naked as Angelena gave him a last check and Dave waited with the helmet. Joyne was not amused. She had never seen Jim naked, and his shrunken chest and protruding paunch, especially the puddle of loose flesh that was his genitalia, only served to remind her that if she ever saw this flesh again it would be empty and dead. That the persona of Jim Brigham would be reborn in a young body was a comfort to him, but not to her. All that he was to her was wrapped up in his age and wisdom, and she would never be free in his presence again.

She remembered the awakening sexuality that had announced itself in the stiffening of Dave's penis every time she approached during his first days. Jim would react the same way. He would have no choice, and at his first erection all the safety he had represented would be destroyed. He would become predatory in that moment, and, knowing this, her girlhood fled her.

Dave was watching her. It was a friendly look, quizzical, even concerned. She saw suddenly the picture of a grim man in his mid-thirties—Ram David

Singh—superimposing itself over Dave's boyish face, and she shivered.

Chandra was watching her, too, but he was merely a young man. The uncanny resemblance and equally uncanny differences between Chandra and Dave caught her unprepared. Suddenly the whole question of identity and the boundaries of the self grew up around her, suffocating her with the weight of possibilities. Her mother looked up and Joyne saw herself thirty more years into life. Questions of I and you that had seemed so stable suddenly burst forth in a maelstrom of uncertainty and she gripped the table before her until pain brought her whirling *self* back to the mundane here-and-now.

Angelena was beside her asking what was wrong and she heard her own voice making foolish excuses about lack of sleep. After a while, they let her alone and she continued to watch as Dave covered Jim's head with the deathmask. It was wrong that her last sight of him should be of the body only, showing nothing of the face where identity resides.

They raised his ancient body, slack now under the influence of drugs, and slipped it through the steel vulva of the S.D. tank. Then the waters (Mother Ganga, Mother of Waters—Gods, how my mind wanders) came rushing in to plunge him back into the sleep that precedes life.

Joyne cried out but the sound never surfaced and no one took heed.

Chapter 28

It would take ten days to imprint Jim's memories into the new clone. After the first day, Nirghaz returned to Raipur; Chandra elected to remain behind. At first he left Dave alone, but after they were drawn together in the general conversations that always sprang up after evening meals, Chandra began to warm toward Dave.

They saw little of one another. After the first tense evening, Dave tended to avoid Chandra, and Chandra was immersed in learning about the project. But on the ninth day of Jim's taping, they met by chance before dinner and Chandra challenged Dave to a game of squash. Dave declined; it would have been no contest and he didn't feel like losing gracefully. "In a year, Chandra. Challenge me then, and I'll whip you down."

They settled on a swim. Joyne had preceded them. She was lying back with her long, wet hair fanned out to dry and seemed to be sleeping. She did not open her eyes until their splashing brought them to her attention. Since Jim's taping had begun, she had avoided them all, and not even Anson and Angelena could comfort her.

Dave would have left her alone when they emerged, but Chandra pulled up a chair next to her and said, "We haven't seen much of you lately."

She smiled back at Chandra, but it was clearly an effort. There were dark stains beneath her eyes. Dave ignored Chandra's insensitivity and asked, "Are you all right?"

She only shrugged.

Undaunted, Chandra ignored Joyne and turned to Dave. "I've been wanting to talk to you."

"What about?"

"About our linked past and Mother's idea that I have your *atman.*"

"You don't believe that."

"I'm not even sure what an *atman* is, but Mother seems convinced; even fanatical."

"So I noticed," Dave said dryly.

"Until a few days ago I didn't know that *Inquiry* was anything more than another foolish tract. Now I find that my parents were wound up in it from the beginning, and yet no one seems to believe in it less than my mother."

"Chandra, you say that you read *Inquiry* before Nirghaz told you about it. Where was that?"

"Poona. In college."

"How did you get hold of it?"

"That was easy enough. It's an underground classic."

"Oh."

"Does that surprise you?"

"Yes, but I suppose it shouldn't."

Joyne had closed her eyes now and to all outward appearances was ignoring them, but Dave felt that she was following the conversation intently.

The wind rustled suddenly among the trees, catching leaves and scattering them about. Joyne shivered, and Dave wondered if it was the wind or something deeper. She had not been the same since they had begun to implant Jim's clone, and he wondered just what she thought of the whole process. She had grown up with it.

More than any of them, it should have been a natural thing for her.

But when Dave had come among them, there had been no Dave before him for comparison. Jim was gaining a new body, but in Joyne's eyes he would never be the same person that he had been before. The gap between his coming youth and his passing age was too great. It would be at least a strain on their relationship. It might even destroy it, and Dave felt strangely sad at the thought.

Dave asked, "Chandra, what do you think of this *atman* business?"

"Perhaps I do have your *atman,* or perhaps I don't, but we share something. Our bodies are identical. . . ."

"As twins are."

"More than that. When I was a child I had dreams that I could not understand. Thinking back on them now, they all fit in with *your* life at the Institute. I dreamed of a much younger Shashi and Nirghaz. I even dreamed of Gopal Choudry, though I never met him: tall, brown hair and eyes, balding, a little round in the stomach. He had a tic; he always rubbed his eyes when he started to say anything he thought might be contradicted."

Dave felt something like cold panic growing within him, but he squelched it mercilessly. "That's Gopal, all right. I'm sure you must have heard Shashi or Nirghaz speak of him."

"Perhaps. A child hears many things that he doesn't remember in later life. Sometimes dreams are made up of the half-understood ideas and concepts that seem to float in the air around a child. Nevertheless, I do not believe that they ever described him to me, nor did I know his name until Nirghaz told me about the resurrection project."

Dave shrugged, hiding his sudden uncertainty. "There may be something to what you say, but according to Shashi the *atman* is not memory, and one does not remember one's previous lives."

Chandra nodded. "True, only an adept would remember, and I certainly am not that. Nevertheless, it bothers me a great deal."

Dave laced his hands behind his head as he rolled over to stare at the sky. Deep blue. Fathomless. Beyond understanding; beyond explanation. But not beyond speculation. There was so much he did not know, and he was only beginning to understand the depths of his ignorance. It troubled him deeply.

After Chandra and Dave had left, Joyne opened her eyes to stare at the same sky. She had overheard it all, of course. It was no comfort to her that those whose faith in the process should have been the strongest had doubts of their own. She sat miserably for a while wrestling with the memory of the Jim who had been, trying without success to reconcile herself to the Jim who would be, and eventually the tears started again.

The lights were on when Nirghaz arrived back from the compound. Shashi looked up when he entered and her eyes were wells of bitterness. "Where's Chandra?" she asked.

"At the compound."

"So he decided to stay. I knew he would."

"For a while. He has to sort it all out in his mind. He has to come to his own conclusions."

"You know what those will be. You don't give someone opium and say, 'It's your decision whether or not to become an addict.' "

"No, and you don't refuse someone the breath of life and say, 'It's not good for you. You should not live.' "

He went into the bedroom and began to pack. Shashi followed him and stopped open-mouthed in the doorway. "You're leaving?"

He saw that she was shocked and it disgusted him. "Yes. That's what you want, isn't it?"

"No, it's not what I want. Whatever gave you that idea?"

"I told Chandra, and now you've lost him."

"And I won't ever forgive you. But I still love you, however angry I am with you now, and I don't want you to leave."

Nirghaz turned his back to her. "Shashi, I had a lot of time to think coming back from the compound. You never stopped loving Ramadav, whatever you told yourself. I always knew that, and I hated bringing him back for fear that you would go to him. You really surprised me, and you don't do that often, when you rejected him.

"Now I understand why. You thought that his *atman* transmigrated. I'll give you that; true or false, you really believe it. You were frustrated in your love for Dave, first by his attitude and later by his death, so you transferred your love from Dave to Chandra."

She slapped him. Her eyes were burning bright and her lips curled back as she spat, "Damn your soul, you're accusing me of incest! Do you hear yourself?"

"No!" They were both shouting now. "I never said that you would take Chandra into your bed, but your misplaced affection is strangling him. It isn't healthy. Your refusal to tell him about the project was nothing more than a clinging refusal to let him go.

"Your emotions are so damned screwed up now that there is no room for me anymore."

"You're still jealous of Chandra."

"Damned right, but now I know why."

He returned to the living room and she followed. He said, "I'll take a room in a hotel downtown."

"Just like that?"

"Just like that. I have to straighten out our financial affairs and give notice at work. I can't just walk out without having people ask questions, and questions are the one thing we can't stand."

"*You* can't stand."

"*We* can't stand, Shashi. The Secret Police may have left us alone, but that doesn't mean that they have forgotten us.

"I'm leaving most of my things here. I'll send for them later. I don't know when."

"I don't want them here."

"I don't give a damn whether you want them here or not! It's still my house."

"I thought it was *our* house."

"So did I. Seems I was wrong."

Chapter 29

NIRGHAZ HAD COME BACK LATE THE night before looking harried. Dave started to ask him what was wrong but thought better of it. He was carrying a suitcase and settled in to one of the empty rooms. That told Dave what he needed to know, and it saddened him to think that Shashi was alone now.

When Dave came down to breakfast, Angelena told him that the imprinting was finished. Within an hour everyone had gathered in the labs. Joyne was there, and when Dave and Angelena came in, she rushed into Angelena's arms crying.

"Baby, what's wrong? You've been acting like this for days. Come on, you've got to talk to me." But Joyne would not talk, and when Angelena had to disengage herself to work on the clone, Joyne stood dumb and miserable in the corner wringing her hands together.

They opened the great steel door to the outer chamber, drained it, and worked their way in to open the inner door. The second chamber was still filled with water and the clone hung there white as a grub.

Nels hooked his hands under its armpits and pulled it out with Dave and Anson helping. It was flaccid; they could hardly handle it, though it weighed less than forty kilograms. Head, arms, fingers, legs, everything akimbo, everything drooping and falling. Joyne had to turn her head away, and even Dave found himself a little sickened by the creature. They laid it on a hospital bed and dried it carefully, then removed the headpiece. It shuddered and drew one stricken breath; then the breathing settled into a shallow, even rhythm.

Angelena checked it with a stethoscope while Nels, Anson, and Dave worked quickly to tape on telemetering devices. It shuddered convulsively, then settled down again. Angelena's eyes were worried; Dave's eyes mirrored the emotion. This was not a routine thing. A moment's inattention on their part could destroy this still-fresh life.

Nirghaz hovered nearby, doing nothing and finding it difficult to remember the promise he had made. Chandra was silent, stricken by the drama of it all. All leads attached, Anson retreated to his computer console and Dave joined him there. The computer would probe more deeply and with greater facility than Angelena could with her simple stethoscope.

Within the frail body, the heart beat a slow, uneven rhythm; the breathing was shallow; the chest hardly seemed to rise and fall at all. The fingers and toes were blue. Its circulatory system had not yet accustomed itself to the sudden surge of gravity.

For three hours they worked.

Anson turned from the console and nodded to his wife. "As nearly as it is humanly possible to establish," he said, "Jim has transferred. The clone will live. It's healthy; there is no sign of defect of any kind."

Nirghaz tensed himself for a confrontation, praying it would not come. Dave said, "There is no question, then?"

"No reasonable question."

Dave nodded. "Okay. Angelena—questions, comments, objections?" She shook her head. "Then there is nothing to stop us from cutting off life support."

Joyne wanted to cry out, wanted to leap forward and stop them, wanted to run, wanted to bury herself in a womb more secure than the one they had just ripped the clone from. She said nothing. She could say nothing, but her fingers tightened around the bedpost until her fingers were white. It was not courage that kept her from crying out. She simply could not.

All this Dave saw as he cut the life support.

No!" The scream finally made its way to the surface, but Dave's hand had already descended. Within the second S.D. tank the oxygen was cut off, and the quiet breathing that still went on in Jim Brigham's ancient body ceased.

It should have been Anson's job, or even Angelena's. Dave had usurped it because if Joyne chose to hate someone for destroying Jim's old body, it was better that she hate him than her parents.

Ten minutes passed, then twenty. Time enough, and time enough again for death to come.

Nirghaz had wandered off, his duty discharged. Chandra remained, fascinated by the white thing lying before him. He looked at it, then looked up at Dave, whose body had been like that so recently, and found a new respect for the man.

Joyne remained in some private world where no one could reach her, though Angelena left the clone to sit beside her and hold her close. Her mind had retreated to a safer, saner place.

From time to time the clone twitched, but mostly it lay back, crushed into the bed by the force of gravity. They all thought of it as "the clone"; it would not become Jim Brigham for them until it spoke. Yet they knew it for what it was and they watched it jealously to see that no harm came to it.

Finally, the time came to remove Jim's old body from the tank.

They broke the seals on the outer door and threw it back. They opened the valves and the water flushed away. Dave dropped through and opened the inner door; Anson hauled up on the umbilicus as Dave dragged up the now-limp body.

Joyne was sobbing softly.

They laid it out on a table and Angelena checked it perfunctorily for life signs. Then Dave covered it with a sheet, and they ignored it.

That night Chandra dreamed of a cabin somewhere in the mountains. The mountains were green and beautiful, the crops were sparse, the living was hard. His father (it was not Nirghaz) was a hard, lean man and he had brothers who worked the land beside him, and then one by one drifted off into their own worlds.

In the dream he lived through an uncertain version of his father's death. He heard him crying out in his death throes, but the words were strangely without meaning.

He woke up cold and sweating, chided himself for childishness, and slept again.

This time he dreamed of ice-locked fjords and a red crabbing boat rigged for a long passage.

Chapter 30

"STAR."

It had been three days since Jim's rebirth. Joyne had recovered some of her composure, but refused to visit Jim during his still-short periods of consciousness.

"Cross."

Dave laid another card face up from the Rhine deck and concentrated on it. "Wave," said Chandra. Dave kept his face impassive and turned up another card. When he had run through the deck, Joyne nodded that she had tabulated the results and Dave shuffled the deck thoroughly and began to deal them slowly, one at a time, face down, while surreptitiously watching Joyne. He was worried for her; yet at the same time he resented her refusal to go to Jim.

For each card that Dave dealt, Chandra made a response, but he was considerably less certain now. Dave ran through the deck, picked it up, and dealt again without shuffling, face up so that Joyne could record how the cards had fallen. Her fingers flew over a portable calculator.

"No question about it," she finally concluded.

"Chandra's responses to the clairvoyance test were negative, but his responses to the telepathy test were positive. Seventeen out of twenty-five right."

"Amazing."

"Hop up, Dave, and let me try." Joyne sat down opposite Chandra and shuffled the cards. She dealt them slowly face up, concentrating on each card as it lay hidden from Chandra by a low barrier.

"Six out of twenty-five," Dave said. "Not statistically significant. Try again." This time he got only four right. "No question. Chandra and I are telepathic together, but he is not telepathic with Joyne—probably is not telepathic with anyone else."

Chandra scooted his chair back and stretched. "That isn't really unusual, is it? After all, we are identical twins, genetically."

"Unusual, yes, but not unheard of. When telepathy can be proved, it is often between identical twins, but it is still rare."

Joyne poured coffee from the pot she had appropriated when they began the experiment and they all relaxed, Dave and Chandra leaning their chairs against the wall in an unconscious parody of one another. "Are you satisfied now, Chandra?" Dave asked.

Chandra shook his head. "No. We have proved nothing, though I will admit that you are marshaling evidence on your side of the argument. You have proved that a mechanism exists, not that it was the instrument that in fact effected the situation."

"Crap. You're carrying skepticism into the realm of pure pigheadedness."

Joyne chuckled and Dave rejoiced silently at that relaxation of sadness. "Would someone mind letting me in on this?"

"Sorry, Joyne," Chandra said. "I've been having dreams in which I am Ram David Singh. When I relate them to Dave, he confirms that they are the record of true events." He called them dreams, but they had become nightmares.

"Interesting, but what does it mean?"

"You know Mother claimed that Ram David Singh's *atman* entered into me when I was in her womb. Dave scoffs, but I am more open-minded than he is."

"Keep an open mind and people will always be throwing garbage in it," Dave interjected.

"A fine way for an ex-scientist to talk. Anyway, I don't discount her story out of hand, and I have been trying to determine whether or not I am remembering a previous life."

Joyne looked troubled, but Dave patted her knee and chuckled. "I told Chandra that he was only heterodyning on my brain because we are genetic identicals, and I proved it to him tonight. We are natural telepaths. True, there have been no overt symptoms, but at night when his waking brain is quiescent, he picks up memories out of my mind. Simple."

"'Simple,' he says. We understand telepathy no better than we understand reincarnation. In fact, they both stand as unproved hypotheses." He held up his hand as Dave started to protest. "Now don't jump on me. What we have in both cases is a series of claimed phenomena. Sometimes these phenomena can be verified, as tonight, but the theory which explains them is either lacking or unprovable. If I choose to believe in *atmans* and reincarnation, I am no less scientific than Dave's uncritical acceptance of telepathy."

Dave shrugged and grinned. "You can't argue with logic, even if it is logical nonsense."

"Do you believe in reincarnation?" Joyne asked. "I mean, do you believe that you inherited the *atman* of Ram David Singh?"

"Now don't you start in," Dave pleaded.

"Hush, Dave. I never met 'Ram David Singh' and I don't care who has custody of his *atman,* or even if he had one. I just wonder what Chandra believes."

"I don't believe anything. I am troubled by dreams of a past that is not my own, and I am seeking an answer to their meaning. Despite Dave's snide remarks, I do have an open mind."

Dave left Chandra and Joyne together and went down to see if Jim was awake. Angelena was there with him.

"Hi, Angi. How's he doing?"

"Oh, Dave. Hi. Fine. He was awake until about a half an hour ago, so don't expect to talk to him until tomorrow morning."

Angelena liked to stay near her patient, though the computer actually kept track of his vital signs. Dave pulled up a chair to join her.

"Angi, I'm worried about Joyne."

"I know, Dave. So am I."

"Do you know what's wrong with her?"

Angelena shrugged. "I suppose. She's very young. All the more so for never having had to face up to death before."

Dave understood that. He was momentarily transported to the Ozark hills, where he had fought his own bitter battles with concepts of life and death, and had come away with a troubled philosophy.

"I wish she would come down and talk to Jim," Angelena said. "Once she hears his voice she will know that he is still the same."

"It must be very strange for her."

"Strange for us all."

After Dave had gone to bed, he lay a long time staring at the ceiling. Joyne had changed during the last week and it was not, in his opinion, entirely for the worse. He felt for her sorrow and he understood it; yet for all that, it had broadened and deepened her. She was no longer the child that she had been.

He dozed; then something awakened him.

He stared wide-eyed into the darkness, confused by sleep. His door swung open, then gently closed again.

There was a soft movement in the room and someone knelt by his bedside. He could not see who it was in the darkness, so he reached out sharply.

Joyne?

"What do you want?" he whispered. His fingers followed her arm up from elbow to shoulder, and to her face. In the darkness he found moisture on her cheeks.

Straightening up, he shook his head to clear away sleep, and her hands found his. They interlaced painfully. Again he asked, "What's the matter?"

"I needed to talk to someone."

"All right. I'm listening," he said gently, though he was surprised that she had come to him.

Almost as if she had read his mind, she said, "I wanted to go to Jim, but I couldn't, and every time I thought of Mum or Dad I could only see them broken and old like Jim was when you pulled him out of the tank. I loved him so much." Then she broke down into sobs.

"He still lives." Dave's hands found her face and turned it toward him, though he could hardly see her in the dim moonlight. "He still lives, and he asks for you. Why don't you go to him?"

"I can't."

Though he disliked saying it, Dave felt compelled to add, "You are hurting him very badly by not going to him."

"I know. That's the worst part of it. I know that he's alive; I know that he wants me to go to him, and I want to go to him, but I can't."

"Why? Because he's young again?"

"Because he has changed; he's not the same person that he was."

"Joyne, you're just looking at the shell. He's the same person that he always was, and you know it."

She shrugged miserably. He would not have seen the motion, but he felt it through his hands.

He considered taking her down to Jim now and forcing her to face the issue, but Jim wouldn't wake up until morning. She needed to see him when he was awake and alert; when the same voice spoke to her and the same kindness came out to enfold her.

"Dave?"

"Yes?"

"You're cold. I can feel it in the way you touch me. What have I done?"

Dave considered his growing irritation with her and replied, "I think it's because you're treating Jim the same way Shashi treats me."

"It's not the same."

"In what way is it different?"

She didn't answer that, and he went on: "You need courage to face it, but we all need courage. The only way to find it is to force yourself, for all the pain it costs, to do the thing that you know needs doing."

Instead of replying, she gently disengaged herself from him. He thought that she was leaving until he realized that she was slipping off her blouse.

"Joyne, are you sure you're ready for this?"

"I'm sure."

Dave wasn't so sure he was ready. There was a skip in logic between her words and her actions that caught him off guard. Yet the adolescent hungers of his new body responded instantly. He had said it to Jim, back before Jim had renewed. "I remember what it was like to be a boy of fifteen. I remember the hungers and the frustrations and I remember how every sensation was fresh and new. But the first time is never good, because there is no experience to guide the body. Such a shame. This time it will be different."

She slipped the covers back and slid in beside him, and it was different.

After a while, Joyne said, "I feel old and young at the same time. That's why I needed you tonight, Dave—you in particular. Because you're old and young at the same time."

"Sometimes I think everyone is."

"Maybe. Do you remember the day of our picnic? Do you remember how I suddenly pushed you off and began to pack up for our return?"

"Of course, but I never figured out why."

"You were talking about things that had happened twenty years ago—before I was born—as if they were yesterday, and for the first time I really understood what you are, age and youth all bound up together. After that, I couldn't react to you. Now I think I've grown up some."

He chuckled. "That seems to be."

"I don't mean that, and you know it."

"No, I know what you mean."

"Dave, will you hate me if I say I've used you?"

"I knew you were using me, and I think I know why."

"Do you really?"

"You tell me, and I'll tell you."

"I . . . I had to have you, young and old together, before I could face Jim, who is old and young together."

"That's what I thought. You'll take him as a lover, won't you?"

"*No!*"

"You don't shock me. Jim is my closest friend."

"No, that's not it. I could never take Jim as a lover."

"Why?"

"Because he'll always be a grandfather to me, no matter what he looks like."

"I think you're mistaken."

"No. No; never Jim."

"That surprises me."

"Did you think that I made love to you just so that I could later make love to Jim? Do you rate yourself that low?"

Dave said nothing and she took his silence, correctly, to mean yes. She stiffened and drew away from him.

"Before you get too mad, Joyne, remember; I didn't stop you. And that's because I love both you and Jim."

"You love me?"

"I think I'm beginning to."

"Because of tonight?" She laughed uneasily.

"No. Because of the person I see you becoming."

She was silent for a moment and he thought that she had started to cry again. Perhaps she had, but when he reached out she came lightly into his arms; and when she buried her head against his neck, it was not with tears, but with love nips that quickly aroused him and started a new round of lovemaking.

Once in his room Chandra slipped out of his clothing, dropped into lotus position, and tried to empty his mind. There was a test of validity to the idea of reincarnation and he was about to try it. He expected failure, for what he was attempting was better suited to the efforts of an adept, but he hoped that his unique history would bring him success.

Thoughts rose unbidden and drifted away. For a time he worried about Nirghaz's break with Shashi, and that set off a long chain of associations. He patiently let them run their course, neither welcoming nor rejecting them, for both are forms of attachment, and attachment is the enemy of silence.

Then there was nothing for a time, in a place that knows no time. And then he was drifting through a labyrinth of shifting images and half-apprehended concepts. He moved at the behest of unseen tides until they coalesced into a firm image.

The concrete was hot beneath his feet and the sky was blue. He felt the warmth of the day, sultry damp heat. He squinted against the glare.

There were hands on either arm and he turned his head to see a soldier in the uniform of the Indian Air Force with an M.P. armband and sidearm. This was the province of Ram David Singh—memories that Dave did not share. It was true, then. He sought to disengage himself from the scene, but could not. He began to struggle.

Behind him a familiar/unfamiliar voice said, "Let him go." The rough hands released him and he turned to face a colonel, who could only be Bhatt. He was short and dark, inclined toward a paunch, and his face looked self-satisfied at this moment. Cold fear shot through Chandra. He fought against the trap he had constructed for himself.

"You two. Come here." The soldiers backed away, clearly puzzled. Chandra tried to cry out, but no sound formed.

Bhatt stopped smiling. "Men, he is trying to escape. Stop him."

No. No!

The soldiers who had held him swung their weapons up; one of them was grinning. A voice—his voice—rang in his ears, shouting, "Bhatt, no! No, no!"

Flash.

Sound.

Impact.

Pain!

The screaming awakened Dave. For a moment he was lost; then he realized that he had dozed off in his own bed still entwined around Joyne. Whether she, too, had dozed or had merely stayed with him, he did not know.

The screams came again. Joyne sat bolt upright and Dave leaped to the floor. The sound had come from Chandra's room.

Anson stuck his head out of his bedroom as Dave reached Chandra's door, threw it open, and found Chandra writhing on the floor with his hands clutched to his chest.

Chapter 31

CHANDRA'S SCREAMING STOPPED AS abruptly as it had started and he went into a deep withdrawal. Dave shook him roughly, to no effect, and Angelena shouldered past him, snapping, "Stop that."

She examined him briefly, then shook her head. "Let's get him down to the lab." Joyne jerked at Dave's arm and pressed his trousers into his hand. He slipped them on absently and helped Nirghaz and Anson lift Chandra's stiff body to the bed while Nels ran for a gurney.

Suddenly, Chandra relaxed and his twisted hands fell away from his chest. His contorted face went slack and Angelena dropped down beside him with her ear to his mouth. "Not breathing," she snapped. She tipped his head back to open his airway and sealed her mouth over his, inflating his lungs four times quickly. Then she felt for his carotid pulse. "No pulse. Damn! Get him back on the floor."

The command obviously made no sense to Nirghaz, so Dave grabbed Chandra's shoulders and dumped him gracelessly onto the rug, then went down opposite Angelena and began chest compressions while she interspersed breaths. Nirghaz stood in silent shock; Joyne went running for more equipment.

Dave and Angelena continued CPR all the way down to the lab, where they hooked Chandra into the same life-support equipment that had been used earlier on Jim.

None of the project members was an M.D. Shashi was and Gopal Choudry had been; the rest of them possessed knowledge in other specialties, but their connection with the project had made them all knowledgeable in general medicine.

"I don't think the problem is medical," Anson said, expressing their consensus. "What were you three doing last night after the rest of us went to bed?"

"Why?" Joyne snapped.

"Because I have only seen this kind of withdrawal after a bad drug experience."

Dave explained about the Rhine test and its results. "Chandra had complained of nightmares in which he remembered my past. We concluded that it was a case of unconscious telepathy."

"No, Dave," Joyne corrected, "you concluded that." And she explained about Shashi's claim that Ram David Singh's *atman* had transmigrated to Chandra at his death. Nirghaz stood holding Chandra's unresponsive hand and offered no comment.

Anson shook his head. "I don't know how that helps us."

"If only he had been taped."

That, of course, was the crux. Chandra had never been taped. If he died, it would be the true death. Joyne shivered in Dave's arms and he patted her shoulder, then moved over to stand beside Nirghaz. "Don't blame yourself, Nirghaz. You only did what you thought was right."

Nirghaz looked up bitterly. "Wrong. I did what

Shashi thought was right. For her sake, I neglected my duties to my son."

There was no comfort that Dave could offer.

Angelena spent the day in vain attempts at diagnosis. Dave had ideas of his own, and spent the day with Anson working up a new program for the computer. Joyne was at his elbow all through his preparations, and he had to explain his intentions.

"When I first started my research into memory taping, the most promising leads I had to follow were out of telepathy research. The basic premise I started with was that everyone was missing one essential point. Researchers were treating telepathy like a biological telephone and searching for the mechanism that made it possible in defiance of all known laws of physics. What struck me was that the messages transmitted were not spoken messages, but of a more basic nature. It was a sending of direct apperceptions, filtered through the observer's senses and concepts, but still not channeled by language. In short, it was the raw material of thought.

"I picked up on experiments in computer-enhanced telepathy and turned them to my own ends. Since the basic research had already been done in telepathy, cloning, and growth stimulation, all I had to do was piece together these seemingly unrelated fields of research and jury-rig a method of physiological resurrection. It took me only nine years to work the bugs out of the process."

Joyne shifted her weight as Dave leaned forward to punch new codes into the computer, then leaned his head back against her again. "What," she asked, "does this have to do with helping Chandra?"

"Since we have the capability to monitor memory, which is just fossilized thought, we can use the same techniques to get a look at what is going on in Chandra's brain right now. That should give us a clue to a cure.

"Unfortunately, there is no way to display what the computer will be able to record."

"Can't you jury-rig some kind of printout?"

"You don't understand. Thought is of an entirely different order than speech. To 'display' thought would require a quantum jump in our understanding of how consciousness adheres to matter. We are at a very primitive stage of knowledge in this field.

"The only way Chandra's thoughts can be apprehended is by implanting them directly into another human mind."

Joyne bit her lip to hold back protest. She had feared as much. "Dave, won't whatever is causing Chandra's withdrawal cause the same withdrawal in whoever goes into mindbridge with him?"

"Possibly—especially if it were someone close to him like Nirghaz. But I doubt that what he is experiencing would have such a powerful effect on a stranger." Even as he said it, though, he was filled with a sense of foreboding that he might be wrong.

Nirghaz would have gone, but Dave refused to allow it, and though the others tried to convince Dave that it was too risky for him, none of them offered to take his place. Knowing his real reasons for taking the risk, he did not blame them.

Whatever was killing Chandra was a demon out of Dave's own past. Something out of those lost weeks that Dave could not remember. If it were hallucination on Chandra's part, Dave would recognize it as such. But if it were something more, something real . . .

He had to know.

Chapter 32

HE PAUSED ON THE EDGE OF A GREAT darkness.

Fear was in him, fear of the unknown, the other, and the self.

There loomed before him a massive portal. Iron gates shut him off from the path before him. Symbols? Or real gates that he or Chandra had once experienced; or both? What significance did they have?

He bade them open and the path lay before him. All around him, colors. Sharp, painful hues he could not name. His body felt strange and he looked down to see that he was a child again.

Whose body? Chandra's or his? As they were identical, he could not say.

A cabin; no, two cabins. Similar and superimposed, they had nevertheless been separated in space and time. One he recognized as the cabin where he had grown to young manhood and he turned his face away from reliving those memories. The other cabin was newer, of bitudobe rather than logs. It really resembled the other very little (as his birthplace faded), except that both were homely and humble. What other similarities they shared, he could not yet know.

He walked to the door and peered in, clinging to the doorway shyly in the manner of a child. Nirghaz was there with Shashi, both engaged in the uninteresting business of living. Their ages put the scene in its place; a childhood memory of Chandra's. And apparently one of little significance, for it quickly faded away.

Images then, shifting subtly into one another. Images without meaning, passing in a parade of nameless faces; identities impinging and retreating too quickly for Dave to understand them.

All images coalesced then into one. Shashi, her *chotie* lifted to let her infant suckle. Yet it was not a child's image of warmth and amorphous security. It was Shashi herself, perceived in detail. Much the age she had been in Dave's last memory before his "death", but sadder, and more constrained. This could not be Chandra's memory, or his. Hallucination? It faded and he did not know.

He was lost then in a maelstrom of concepts and reactions, angers and lives, all directed at a world that was not his own. Brief bits of memory from Chandra's life—disconnected, they dazzled like gems, but Dave could get no coherent picture from them. He felt himself slipping away, being carried like a chip on the waves of some great ocean; then he was one with the waves, part of the whole and distinct only for disconnected moments. He fought back, concentrating on his body lying in a bed in the lab. Find his hand. Feel his hand. Joyne's hand would be there as a sure anchor to reality.

It was. Still immersed, he found those fingers and squeezed to hang on to *now* while he plunged back into Chandra's mind.

This was getting him nowhere. He concentrated on

Chandra as he had known him in their few days together. Not only on the body so like his, but on the person who had inhabited it. And he found himself staring across a room at . . . *himself*. Of course; their first meeting, seen now through Chandra's eyes. He felt the hostility of that meeting and the angry thought: *So this is the one whose* atman *I have supposedly inherited.*

There were two shocks from the recent past still resonant in Chandra's mind. Dave held onto the moment and dredged into Chandra's memory for them, superimposing them onto the now-frozen scene of their meeting lest he lose himself again in a labyrinth of simultaneous time. Nirghaz had told him (*Had told Chandra! Must retain my identity.*) that *Inquiry* was a true statement and that he and Shashi were not what they seemed. That was the former shock and in its way the greater. But the latter shock was more subtly damaging. Shashi, a few hours later. While Nirghaz waited outside, she told Chandra of Ram David Singh's death and of the *atman* that had entered into her at that time. He did not believe, but neither could he truly disbelieve, and he left her with a feeling of unnameable loss.

Dave let the memories go and his ruminations drew him back from the maelstrom in Chandra's mind to some other place where the peace of black oblivion dwelled. There he contemplated.

These incidents were clues to causes, but not the causes themselves. He must hesitate no longer.

He plunged again into the surging images, and sought out a room, Joyne, himself, and the Rhine testing; having found it, he stayed with Chandra after Dave (*he!*) and Joyne left, followed him in his ruminations on life and his supposed shared identity with Ram David Singh, whom Chandra considered a different person from the present Dave. (*Careful,* Dave warned himself. *To be caught in that path of reasoning is the straight way to madness.*)

He followed Chandra as he went into lotus position, felt the peace of an emptying mind and then the dream . . .

. . . and rose up screaming from the bed in the transfer room. He felt the concern of his friends around him momentarily, but as his body fell back against the bed he abandoned it again for that limbo where neither the "real" world nor Chandra's thoughts could penetrate.

For a time he bided quiet, until the terror had passed. So that was the dream that had sent Chandra screaming into madness. It had seemed so real. Chandra could have built it up subconsciously from what he knew of Ram David Singh's last day, but . . .

But what if it were a true memory? Only a few weeks ago (*when he had been Ram David Singh; two decades as others measured time, but only weeks to him*) he would have scoffed, but he was no longer so certain.

His own words to Jim in the garden rose up in his mind. "There is so little that we really know."

He was terrified. He longed to return to his body, to bury himself in Joyne's willing flesh and let all demons die and be damned. But the pull of self crying out for identity was stronger.

He would investigate the source of the mystery; trembling, he set out.

Down the torrent of days, backward now. From young manhood to youth to infancy; past the image of Shashi that no infant could have experienced; back to the mad, screaming pain that was Chandra's (*and every man's*) induction into sensate life; back deep into the moist, warm, secure, all-enveloping womb.

There where time was not, and no space, no self, and no other; there he floated.

And there he was quickened. Something, some *thing*, came flooding in to fill him.

Atman? A mere word. It *was;* he felt it, experienced it, and no word would ever be sufficient to capture it.

Again he plunged back, ignoring the madness of the sights that appeared before him. Those would come again later. God help him, he could only return by this same route.

Past the madness and into familiar territory now. Flying swiftly backward down his own memory, through his days at the Institute, his days as a student, his days as a sailor. He saw his father rise up from his deathbed and stalk backward into younger age, as he himself grew younger. His mother lived again, and Pat, his elder brother. Then he, too, was being suckled, and then his birth pain, and then warm oblivion.

He could plunge back further. He could, but he hesitated.

What would he find? Oblivion? The formless stuff of I-am-not-yet; that nether reflection of death. Or other lives already lived, down a long dusty corridor into the mists of creation.

He stood at the portal of a great mystery and drew back. He had not the courage to go further.

Now he was born, and now he was weaned, and now he was growing. He saw his father die again and rushed, faster still this time, upward from youth to experience. College, Poona, the Institute, Shashi and sweet liaison. Then Deliac and the project nearing completion. His memory was slowing now as he approached the last taping.

There is no way around. I can only go through. But it is not right that Chandra should bear my burden for me. If I live and if he lives, I will thank him for giving me back this fragment of my life.

He rose up groggy from the bed where he had been taped and gathered the tapes and his letter to Jim Brigham. Jim would understand him, if anyone did. Jim he could trust with his life.

He relived the weeks that followed, knowing yet not

knowing that this was not the reality of here-and-now. Again they began Nirghaz's resurrection, and again it was interrupted. Imprisonment. Nirghaz's suicide. The project renewed. Drawing Nirghaz's pale new body up.

Time was slowing now, and the dread of what was to come grew up in Dave until it nearly smothered him.

Bhatt stood in the doorway. He smiled.

The warmth of the parade ground. The soldiers, one smiling.

The fear and the pain!

Chapter 33

DAVE AWOKE DISORIENTED. HE FELT A presence and an unaccustomed warmth. It was Joyne. He was in his own bed; morning sun through the window had awakened him, and Joyne was lying against his back with her cheek against his neck and one arm limply around him. He stirred and she awoke, looked closely into his eyes for one terrified moment, then embraced him fiercely, kissing him and crying.

"Hey!" After a moment he disentangled himself and grinned. "Later, kid. For sure. But now, what happened?"

He shook his head to clear the cobwebs, then added, "How is Chandra, and what day is it?"

"Friday. You made your mindbridge yesterday morning and it lasted seven hours." She swallowed as if the memory were hard for her. "Once you grasped my hand and once you jerked and moaned, but otherwise you lay there just like you were dead for seven hours. Angelena even rigged up life-support equipment, but you never quite stopped breathing. Then, all of a sudden, both you and Chandra leaped up screaming.

We had a hell of a time restraining you both, especially with Chandra all tangled up in his life-support equipment. Then you both collapsed as suddenly as you had jumped up. After that you both drifted into a normal sleep, and Chandra was breathing and his heart was beating again.

"After Mum had monitored you for an hour, she said that you were normal but exhausted and I insisted that they bring you here. Now what happened to you?"

"Would you believe it's a long story? And I am not sure yet what it all meant, but I'll know more after I've talked with Chandra." He kicked his feet over the side and scrambled for his clothing.

"He may not be awake yet," she cautioned.

"Yes, he is; he awakened when I did."

He shrugged into his shirt and rose, only to see Joyne's face frozen in an expression of terror. He dropped quickly back beside her and took her into his arms. "Hey, Joyne, it's not that strange. We shared our lives as no two people have ever done before, and we were latent telepaths even before that. I can sense Chandra's alertness filling the house now, but that's all. And I'm sure that even that much awareness will fade over the next few weeks."

She fought back her tears. "Dave, I didn't realize how precious you are to me until I thought I had lost you."

He could think of no words adequate for the situation, so their trip to the lab was somewhat delayed.

When they entered the lab, Chandra had already looked up, sensing them coming, and he was smiling. All of the coldness that had lain between them was gone. Dave reached out and touched fingertips with his son, who was also his father, and they both grinned.

"How do you feel?"

"Marvelous, Dave." And without waiting for the next question, Chandra went on: "It is gone."

Joyne was puzzled. "What's gone?"

"Ram David Singh's *atman*. I had bottled it up for twenty years until I was no longer even aware of its existence, and when I let it loose that night it choked me insensible."

Joyne looked frightened again. *Well, hell, no wonder,* Dave thought. "Not *atman,* Chandra. Whatever *it* was, it should not be called by a name that carries with it thirty-five hundred years of religious speculation. *It* existed, as surely as the *I* which drove me to these experiments in the first place. But we don't understand it, so let's not give it a name and pretend that we do."

"As you will." Joyne was surprised to see Chandra deferring so readily. Whatever childish competition had been between them was gone now.

Dave was lost in thought. They had shared memory, yet he knew little more about Chandra than he had before. A few dissociated images and a general feeling. Nothing more. He suspected that Chandra had shared the same from his life.

But his own memories from the last taping to his execution were firmly implanted. He had not got them secondhand; he had lived them. They were inextricably part of him.

And he did not understand that at all.

"Chandra, do you remember much from my life, especially after the last taping?"

"Not much. I remember it as something from a dream."

So. As he had suspected.

Joyne was pulling shyly at his finger, the most childlike mannerism he had yet seen in her. Yet it did not seem inappropriate at that moment. "What will you do now?" she asked.

"I have to go see Shashi."

"Why? She hates you."

Looking at Joyne, Dave saw a curious mixture of jealousy and protectiveness, and smiled. "Nevertheless, I must go to her."

Joyne's hand on his arm was no longer merely

companionable. It was a compulsion trying to restrain him and she forgot Chandra's presence for the moment.

"Don't go to her. Stay here with us."

He shook his head, and she screwed up her face in petulance. "She is the past; I am the future."

It was true, and he would return quickly. He laid his arm across her shoulder, smiling. "That you are, Joyne. But a wise man makes peace with both."

It took most of the day to reach Raipur, and Dave walked from the station to the bungalow where Nirghaz and Shashi had raised Chandra. He knew it when he saw it, a fleeting recognition out of Chandra's memory, but nothing more than that. He stared at it for a long time, but it was only a house. Whatever significance it had for Chandra, it did not have for him. That was as he had expected it would be, but he would never again be as sure of himself as he had been before.

Besides, he was stalling.

He knocked. No one answered, and after a while he tried the door. It was unlocked.

The living room was painfully neat. That was Shashi for you. He called out, but she did not answer.

He didn't think that she would leave the door open if she were not home, so she was probably in the lab. Dave let himself out into the yard and found himself in a flower garden of riotous color. He touched the petals of a rose that someone—Shashi, of course—had cultivated lovingly, and a phrase from Tagore came back to him:

Be not ashamed, my brothers, to stand before
*   the proud and the powerful*
With your white robes of simpleness.
Let your crown be of humility, your freedom
*   the freedom of the soul.*
Build God's throne daily upon the ample
*   bareness of your poverty*

*And know that what is huge is not great and
    pride is not everlasting.*

That was Shashi.

He still loved her. The realization came as a surprise
to him and he was rooted to the spot by a sudden rush
of memories. A tear even formed in his eye, but he
brushed it away. The Shashi that he remembered was
twenty years gone, and this Shashi was much harder
and colder than that one had been.

This Shashi—that Shashi. Ram David Singh and
Dave Singer. It all seemed so foolish, suddenly.
Standing quietly in the sunlight, he realized in a
moment of transcendent intuition that there was an
essence, an identity, some *thing* behind the *I* which
motivated all his actions, and that essence remained, no
matter what external changes took place.

It was not a soul that transcended the flesh to remain
in undivided selfness throughout eternity, nor an *atman*
that was reborn through long cycles of lives only to
eventually lose its selfness in selflessness. Though men
of high thought and goodwill had brought these specu-
lations to complex and subtle fruition in the name of
religion, they were both far short of reality.

Yet identity remained. The senses might be fooled,
the flesh might decay, but the *I* remained the first and
last experience, and consciousness the only true verifia-
ble reality.

Perhaps it was inviolable, or perhaps it was extinguished with death. He did not know, but in acknowledging his ignorance he took the first step toward
finding out. And now he had eternity for the search.

Shashi was wrong, but she had not been without
wisdom.

And he, in his narrow materialism, had also been
wrong. Yet his error had led to searching, and only by
searching could one find. Shashi's way of acceptance
was the way to dusty death and nothing more.

The moment passed, but it left behind some of the

sweetness of the golden sunlight. He walked on to the separate lab. Shashi was singing softly inside, a simple tune of *bhakti,* devotion. He watched her through the open doorway, her hands busy with vials and tubes as she set up still another experiment, still searching for a cure to the barrenness that plagued the land she loved. This was her way to combat sadness, and it was good. The work was worthwhile, and he respected her for it.

She sensed his presence and turned. He saw her age and saw past her age, and he smiled.

She was wary, but then she stepped up to look more closely at him.

"You've changed," she said.

"Yes. People do."